FRANK
Finds
GRACE

A Novel

Vicki Machoian

VICKI MACHOIAN

ISBN 978-1-64468-017-9 (Paperback)
ISBN 978-1-64468-018-6 (Digital)

Covenant Books, Inc.
11661 Hwy 707
Murrells Inlet, SC 29576
www.covenantbooks.com

To my mother who had the gift of instilling confidence.

The Forward

If you hear of someone finding grace, you most likely assume they've had an experience connecting with God. This is not one of those stories.

1

The Madisons

William Madison was a handsome man, that's for sure, but many thought Henrietta Wilburne married below her station. After all, he was a tradesman. Henrietta, however, was more than a pretty face, and she knew William was more than a good-looking man. She recognized nobility in the character of the carriage maker. She loved him for his innate kindness and his integrity. He loved her. So they were married on a beautiful afternoon in the middle of May.

William Madison was also a visionary, always looking for new ways to improve the appearance and function of his carriages. He had been taught well by his father. His craftsmanship along with his integrity and creative thinking made the Madison Carriage Company the most successful in Pennsylvania. Although not members of Philadelphia's high society, the Madisons lived well. William and Henrietta had two children who enriched the joy of their marriage. When their first child was a son, William relaxed knowing the family business was good for another generation. He never forgot his father's good fortune to inherit the company because Mr. Bronson, the original owner, didn't have an heir. Their son, Frank, was very young when William and Henrietta discovered he learned quickly and showed uncommon dexterity. When Frank started tinkering with left over scraps of wood his father began teaching him the trade. It wasn't long before he could cut and finish carriage pieces, and William knew he could count on him to make reproductions with exactness. When their next child was a daughter, he was happy that his adored wife would have a little girl to dote on. (Like their daughter Sophie didn't have *him* wrapped around her little finger.)

Frank had a diversity of interests and talents, one of which was sometimes a frustration to his father when he often had to drag him back from the livery because of his love of horses. Fortunately, as Frank matured, his father began to recognize that his interest in horses was more than a childhood fascination and decided to encourage it. William was impressed with how much his son was learning during his time at the livery, and he began to realize Frank was enthusiastic about sharing his knowledge of horses. Therefore, he negotiated a partnership with Sid Tillman, the owner of the livery. When a carriage was ordered, Frank could encourage the customer to purchase trained horses along with their carriage. It was a smart business practice for both their carriage company and the Tillman Livery Stables. Frank was surprised when at age eighteen his father sent him to a local college to learn accounting and business practices, and then put him in charge of the finances. When Frank was twenty, Mr. Madison sent him to several neighboring states to expand their territory. Once while delivering a carriage to a customer in Virginia, Frank discovered the excellent quality of the hardware produced by the Richmond Brass Works. This is where our story actually begins.

2

Frank

He felt something brush across the back of his legs as he was loading the last box of brass fittings into the wagon. It sent a thrill through him that made his heart jump. Frank turned to see a girl walking down the street in a pine green muslin dress and a large straw sunbonnet. *It must have been her skirt. But why did the touch of her skirt cause such a reaction in me? Odd.* He felt compelled to watch her. The way she moved reminded him of the dancers in the ballet—graceful. Her skirt swayed gently as she walked. There was an ease in her gate that made her whole body flow in one fluid motion. *Not calculated to attract attention,* he thought. Since her back was to him and she was wearing a Southern style sunbonnet, he couldn't discern her age or her appearance. Still, because of his physical reaction to the touch of her dress, she intrigued him. She was tall for a woman, accentuating the slim but nicely formed lines of her figure. His gaze lingered for a moment more until she turned the corner and was out of sight. Frank returned to the task of readying his wagon for the trip back to Philadelphia, still puzzled by his strange reaction to the touch of the girl's skirt; disappointed that he hadn't seen her face. He was rarely distracted when traveling to deliver a carriage or obtain supplies, yet this experience lingered in his thoughts long after the girl disappeared from sight.

He reflected several times on the incident during his trip home, wishing he had seen her face. The graceful way she moved, and his reaction to the touch of her dress intrigued him. He considered the smiles of the men who nodded and tipped their hats as they passed her. His guess was that she was attractive but felt disappointed that he would never know. The next day, passing through the capital city, he was pleased to see the streets bustling with so many Madison carriages. Life was good.

*****

"Frank, did you see this article in the paper?" said his father, as he slapped the newspaper with the back of his hand. "A company in New York has invented a device to make a carriage ride smoother. It sounds interesting. They are going to introduce it at the trade fair at the end of the month. I think we should go up there and check it out."

Frank leaned over the back of the couch to look at the article. "You're right, it does look interesting."

William Madison always had his eyes open for anything that would improve the quality of their carriages. Frank recognized the value of this characteristic in his father and attributed to it their overwhelming success. Well, that and the standard of fine craftsmanship that had been passed down from his grandfather. Although his father was a master craftsman, Frank was grateful he had been sent to college to study accounting and then put in charge of the finances. Their profits increased, and he felt as though he was making a valuable contribution. However, Frank attributed the major part of the success of their business to the integrity of their work and his father's forward thinking.

"Did I hear you say you were going to New York?" inquired Henrietta Madison, as she was coming from the kitchen.

"Yes, I think Frank and I should go up there to a trade show. I'm interested in a new invention being introduced there."

"Well, you better not plan to leave Sophie and me behind," responded his wife. "Think of all the shopping we could do. Sophie could get her gown for the debutante ball. They get the latest fashions in New York weeks before we see them here in Philadelphia, and we could go to the theater. It would be a waste of a trip for you two to just go up there for a trade show."

"I suppose you are right, my dear," responded Mr. Madison, smiling at Frank. "I guess we are due for a family outing."

"Sophie, did you hear that?" said his wife, as she flew up the stairs like a woman half her age.

"Oh, Mama!" shrieked Sophie when she heard the news. "Can I get my ball gown in New York?"

"Of course," her mother assured her. "That's the reason we are going," she exclaimed, completely forgetting about the trade show. Frank, hearing his mother and sister's excited chatter, smiled. Unless men were two sheets to the wind, they never outwardly engaged in such happy excited conversation.

One evening, a week before their scheduled departure, it didn't take long for the dinner conversation to turn to the planned trip.

"I'm sorry to put a damper on this conversation," said Mr. Madison. "There is a good possibility we are going to have to cancel this outing."

"Oh no," responded Henrietta. "Why?"

"Because, my dear, I received a notice from the mill this afternoon. The machine that was weaving the upholstery for the Bennett's carriage broke down causing a three-day delivery delay. As a result, we won't be able to finish their carriage before we need to leave for New York."

"But, Mother, my ball gown," cried Sophie.

"Yes, Mr. Madison, there must be something we can do," pleaded Henrietta.

"I can stay and finish the upholstery," suggested Frank. "You don't really need me to attend the trade show. It would be a shame for Sophie to miss getting her ball gown in New York, Father." He gave his sister a quick wink. Her face lit up with a grateful smile that warmed Frank's heart.

"I suppose you are right," lamented Mr. Madison. "Are you sure you wouldn't mind?"

"Not at all," Frank assured his family.

During the next few days of preparation, Frank took more notice of his sister. She had grown from being a pesky nuisance into a strikingly beautiful young woman. He reflected on her joy at being able to buy her ball gown in New York and was glad to be able to make sure she wouldn't be disappointed; confident it would make her the prettiest girl at the ball.

Perfectly content with the arrangement for Frank to stay home, he and his father settled into their normal routine. His mother and Sophie, on the other hand, were daily in a state of agitation about what clothes to pack and how much money they should take. And, would the weather continue to be like this? It had been raining every day for the past four days and it was only two days before they would be leaving. The miserable weather was making everyone fearful that similar weather in New York would ruin their activities or even require the trip to be canceled after all. But much to their relief, it cleared up the next day.

There were so many suitcases stacked up by the front door Frank was wondering if he misunderstood they would only be gone for six days.

"Oh, I was so afraid that the rainy weather would spoil everything," reflected Mrs. Madison, while they were waiting for Mr. Madison to bring the carriage around. "Thank goodness it has stopped." Everyone shared her relief. Adding to their excitement, the morning was bright, sunny, and unseasonably warm.

His mother and sister were so excited about the good weather and all the activities they had been discussing, Frank knew, as he waved goodbye at the train station, his father would be listening to a constant chatter of all the wonderful things they would be doing and the planning and replanning of how it was all going to be accomplished.

After seeing his family off, Frank returned home to change his clothes and go to the shop to work on the Bennett carriage. As he entered the house he realized the family's excitement must have indeed rubbed off on him. He became aware of how different the empty house felt.

*****

The upholstery fabric had been delivered earlier than expected, so late the next day Mr. Bennett came to take his carriage home.

He was so pleased with it he was discussing the purchase of a buggy when a constable entered the shop. From the look on the man's face, Frank knew immediately something was wrong.

"Are you Mr. Madison?" the man inquired.

"I'm Frank Madison," he responded.

"May I have a word in private?" he requested.

"Of course, just one moment," said Frank.

He finished hitching up the team of horses, and just before Mr. Bennett's departure, Frank said, "Well, Mr. Bennett, if you are sure you want the buggy, I'll get started on it right away. The construction shouldn't take long once my father returns."

"All right," responded Mr. Bennett. "Let's go forward with it."

As Mr. Bennett's carriage pulled away, Frank invited the constable into the office.

"I'm afraid I come bearing very sad news," he said. "There was a train derailment. A good many of the passengers were killed. Your family, I'm sorry to report, was among those lost."

It took Frank a few minutes to process this information. He stared at the man in disbelief. *My family lost? Does he mean they are dead? Can they really all be dead?* He sat down.

"The tracks had been inspected after the rain, of course," explained the constable. "However, there was a place that looked okay to the inspectors but gave way while the train was traveling over it. Several cars turned over, and then were crushed by others crashing into them. It's the most terrible tragedy the railroad company has ever encountered. They are still trying to identify most of the victims. An uninjured passenger, who owns one of your carriages, recognized your father when the family boarded the train. Also, a business card was found in your father's pocket, so your family was one of the first to be identified. I'm very sorry to be the bearer of such regrettable news."

"Thank you," responded Frank, still in a daze. *Thank you?* he thought. *The man just told me my whole family has been killed.* But there wasn't anything else he could think to say.

"Is there anyone else I should notify?" asked the constable.

"No, no one."

Frank sat there for a long time after the constable left. He didn't know what to think. He didn't know what to feel. His family gone! It seemed like a bad dream. "There has to be a mistake about my family. Dear God, please let it be a mistake."

Some people came into the shop.

"Hello, is anyone here?" they called out. Aroused from his stupor, Frank called back, "Sorry, but we are closed for the day." He couldn't bring himself to face them. He supposed they left when he heard the door close. It was dark by the time he became aware of his surroundings again. He got up, locked the door of the shop, and went home. Once he entered the empty house, the full realization of what had happened overcame him and he wept.

*****

He was disturbed by a noise. As he woke up, he became aware that he was lying on his bed still in his work clothes. There was that noise again. It took him a few minutes to realize it was someone knocking on the door. Frank dragged himself down stairs. The man was a stranger.

"Are you Mr. Madison?" he asked. Frank was about to say no when he realized the man was referring to him.

"Yes, I guess I am," he finally responded.

"I'm from the coroner's office," he said. "We have the bodies of your family at the morgue. I was wondering where you want us to send them."

Frank couldn't comprehend what the man was asking. "What?"

"The bodies of your family. Is there a particular funeral home you want them sent to?"

"Oh," answered Frank. "The one on Second Avenue, I guess. I can't remember the name."

"That's the Kettner Funeral Home. I'll have them contact you when they are in possession of the bodies."

Frank felt like strangling the man. *Bodies? Those are my parents and my sister you are talking about,* he thought, closing the door in his face, his presence being a confirmation that this was more than a bad dream.

The next few days were a blur. He woke up one morning aware that he was hungry, still in his work clothes, and sporting an almost full-grown beard. He threw himself on his knees and pleaded for help, knowing that without it he would be lost. He got up feeling a small amount of energy returning to his spirit. He bathed, shaved, dressed himself, and went downstairs to get something to eat. He was famished. After rummaging around in the kitchen, he found a somewhat withered apple and some stale bread. The ice in the refrigerator was melted so the milk was sour, but a small jar of orange juice was still good so he drank that. Where was the housekeeper? After wandering aimlessly around the house, he picked up the pile of mail by the front door and discovered several notes. One was from the Kettner Funeral Home requesting instructions. It was two days old. The others were from the newspaper boy requesting money, and the housekeeper offering sympathy and wanting instructions. Frank forced himself to the funeral home to make arrangements. The other things could wait.

His grief was so profound that putting his family to rest was a nightmare. He never imagined how much was involved when people die. The need to think clearly in spite of his overwhelming sorrow was almost more than he could handle. He prayed for help on a daily basis. Somehow, with the assistance of his father's solicitor and, perhaps, heaven, he managed.

It was a week after the funerals and settling all the legal matters before Frank was able to go back to the shop, but he still couldn't work. Everything reminded him of his loss. He declined new jobs but forced himself to recognize his obligation to Mr. Bennett. It was hard working alone with such a heavy heart. There was no joy in the work and too many reminders of all that was lost. He was eventually able to finish the buggy, grateful for Mr. Bennett's patience when he understood the circumstances. A few weeks after completing the Bennett buggy, he attempted another new carriage on his own. It proved a disaster. He missed his father's companionship and skills. His heart ached for his beautiful sister's life being cut short, and he missed the sound of his mother's voice and presence which were the binding essence of home and family. Finally, he decided to sell everything—the business, the house; everything.

The West is being settled. I'll go out there and start a new life, he thought, and assuaged his grief by throwing himself into the preparation of this endeavor.

3

A New Life

Frank was pleased that the money he received from the sale of his estate would allow him plenty of time to explore a new future. He bought two horses from his friend, Sid Tillman. The one he named Rochester was one of the finest riding horses he had ever seen, and the other was a sturdy pack horse with a broad back he named Penny. He purchased all the supplies he thought he would need to get to the other side of the Appalachians where he hoped to find a town and restock. His spirits lifted during this preparation. At first, he felt guilty not to be carrying on the family business. However, the memories of what was lost still weighed heavily on his spirit. The empty house haunted him. Trying to make a good quality carriage without his father proved impossible. Thus, his decision to go West and completely change his life gave him some impetus to look forward. This was going to be an adventure and he hoped that new experiences would help him heal.

One night, at the end of his first week of travel while lying on the ground staring at the night sky, Frank reflected on his circumstances. On his trips to deliver carriages, he sometimes spent a night or two like this, but he knew those were temporary. *This may be my way of life from now on,* he thought. *My future is certainly going to be very different from my past.* Still, he was not regretting his decision.

*****

As he came to, Frank realized he was injured but still alive. When he and Rochester were falling down the side of the mountain, he was sure it was to his death. His right cheek was stinging and his shoulder hurt. He put his hand on his aching cheek and felt a long cut, but it didn't seem to be bleeding. However, he could see blood was still soaking his shirt. He tried to think about his situation. *It isn't good.* The pain in his right shoulder was excruciating, and there wasn't much strength in his arm. He saw Rochester at the bottom of the ravine. Dead. Frank was saddened by this loss; Rochester had been such a good horse. He looked up and saw that because the tether had come loose, Penny was still standing on the trail. At least he hadn't lost everything, again. He slowly climbed down the tree, working his way to the ground, and took off his shirt, tying it around his shoulder and arm in an effort to staunch the bleeding. It helped some, but he was still losing blood. Weak and dazed, he was finally able to make it back up to where Penny was standing.

"Thank you for not running off. You're a good girl." He gave her a gentle pat, grabbed her reins, and started walking. His only choice was to keep following the trail down the mountain. He was grateful to be going downhill. He hoped he could find help before he bled out. Toward the bottom of the mountain he found a cave and, with considerable effort, pulled Penny's pack off and pushed it into the cave, grateful not to have passed out from the pain and the loss of blood. Then he put some branches in the cave's opening. *With any luck, I can come back in a few days and find my belongings still here.*

"Okay, girl," he said, as he draped himself on Penny's back. "I hope you're smart enough to follow this trail the rest of the way down this mountain and, dear God, please let me find help." Frank didn't remember getting off the mountain. When he came to, Penny was walking across a valley meadow.

Maggie Hartman saw the man draped over the neck of a horse crossing the meadow. She knew something was wrong.

"Bill, there's a horse coming toward the house," she hollered to her husband. "There's a man on its back, but he ain't upright."

Bill looked up from the wood he was chopping and spotted the horse. Putting down the ax, he ran out to meet it. Frank was only semi-conscious when he felt someone grab Penny's bridle and stop her gait. He had never been so happy to see another human being.

From the look of his shirt, Bill could tell the young man had lost a lot of blood. His eyes were dazed and he was on the verge of passing out.

"Son, what on earth happened to you?" he asked, as he took control of the reins.

"My horse lost his footing," Frank answered, just as he lost consciousness again.

*****

Frank became aware that he was hungry and lying on a comfortable bed. He smelled bread baking.

"Well, you're coming back to us, I see." It was the voice of a woman. He opened his eyes. Maggie was standing over him with a smile on her face. She was a pleasant-looking woman with graying hair and a cheerful voice.

"Where am I?" he asked.

"This here is the Hartman spread. You was a might torn up when you got here, young man. Glad you're finally coming around."

Frank could tell as he became more alert that his shoulder and face were bandaged. "Yeah, it seems I should thank you for your help."

"We had a tricky time getting you sewed up, that's for sure. My husband Bill's had experience with animals, but it's the first time he's had to sew up a human. I think he done a right nice job myself."

"I appreciate your help very much," repeated Frank. "I'm sure I'd be dead without it."

"I suppose you would be," responded Maggie. "You musta lost a lot of blood. You've been out nigh on to three days. Are you hungry?"

"Starving."

"Yeah, I figured as much. I got some oatmeal on the stove and some bread just came out of the oven."

Frank couldn't remember being so thankful for food. He didn't remember anything after eating. Every once in a while he was aware of his head being lifted and liquid going down his throat, experiencing both pain at the movement and gratitude for his thirst being quenched. One day he was aware of the sun shining on his face. Gradually, full consciousness returned.

That night he told Bill and Maggie Hartman about the loss of his family and his decision to find a new life.

"I'm more than grateful for your hospitality. I owe you my life," he said, feeling lucky to have been taken in by such kind people.

"A body can't call himself a Christian if he ain't willing to help out his fellowmen now, can he?" responded Maggie. "What's your name son?"

"Frank Madison"

"You said something about a horse falling. Did you have another horse? The one you rode in here on doesn't have any signs of being injured," inquired Bill.

"Yes, the horse I was riding is dead. One of the best horses I've ever seen. I was coming down the back side of the mountain on the trail from Woodsfield when my horse stepped on a soft spot and we went down. A tree stopped my fall, but Rochester, the horse I was riding, didn't make it. How far back would that be, do you know? I left my gear in a cave and hope it's still there and that I can at least retrieve my saddle bags. All my money is in them."

"We are only a mile from where that trail comes off the mountain," Bill told him. "When you get your strength back, we'll go lookin' for your things."

"I don't want to put you folks out any more than I have. I'm moving West. I'm going to need another horse. Is there somewhere around here that sells horses?"

"This here's a horse ranch. When you're up to it, you're welcome to pick out whatever horse you want," said Bill.

It was another week before Frank could actually remain conscious for a whole day. He was gradually able to sit up for a while and eat meals with Bill and Maggie. Then he began to spend some time walking around for a little while every day. The cut that was high on Frank's shoulder extending to his chest was deep and was affecting the strength and movement of his arm. *I sure hope this isn't a permanent disability.* It worried him to think of being an invalid. He had started out on this adventure willing to face whatever came his way but, at twenty-two, he never considered being disabled. He was hoping he had the kind of courage to deal with that eventuality, even if it meant he would have to give up his desire to explore a new life out West. He wondered what his face would look like when he took the bandage off, but tried not to think about it too much. As his body healed, Frank began to participate more in life on the Hartman Ranch.

*****

While he was growing up, Frank's friend Sid Tillman taught him how to care for horses and what to look for in an animal to determine its health and strength. He taught him to discern those characteristics that would make it a good carriage horse. But as he began to spend more time with Bill Hartman, it didn't take him long to realize there was a lot more to learn. Bill shared more information about horses than Frank knew existed. Bill was a second-generation horse trainer. He bred, raised, and trained horses for the cavalry but also knew how to doctor them.

The horses on the Hartman Ranch were a mixture of wild horses and German Friesian. As he became familiar with the horses, Frank found an excellent animal to replace Rochester. Bill taught him how to domesticate, train, and form a relationship with the animal.

"You want to form a good bond with your horse so it will become a partner," Bill said. "When you're alone in the wilderness, there's not much more valuable than your horse. He's your best friend," he explained. "So training him is the next best thing to raising him from a colt." Rochester was a well-trained horse when Frank bought him, so this was a new experience for him. The first of many.

"I hope when we find Rochester my saddle bags are still there Bill, or I won't be able to pay you for the horse," he said one evening as they were sitting on the porch after dinner. "I didn't have the presence of mind to take my money pouch, so if it's gone, I'll be penniless." *Now there's a depressing thought.*

"You're welcome to stay and work here for a while. That way you can work off the price of the horse. Anyway, Maggie and I have takin a likin' to you," answered Bill.

"Thanks, I'll do that, even if I do find my money," responded Frank. He was discovering that the Hartmans were pleasant Christian people who treated him with such loving kindness, he couldn't help but to start feeling better about life. He loved all Bill was teaching him about horses, and he realized there was a lot he needed to learn about the new way of life he was undertaking.

Early one morning about a week later, Bill and Frank set out in a wagon with Penny in tow in an attempt to retrieve Frank's belongings. The trail up to the cave was too narrow for a wagon, so once they got to the mountain they would have to hike up. Frank had been praying almost daily that his gear and saddle would be untouched. Maggie told him, because there was a better passage further south, the trail he came down was seldom used which gave him hope.

On their way, Frank talked about his family. Bill listened. As he learned more about Frank's family, he wondered if it was possible for this young man to ever get over such a complete loss. Anyone would grieve the loss of their family, but listening to Frank, Bill realized Frank's had been especially close and loving. His heart went out to him, and he prayed he would one day find someone like his Maggie to bring joy back into his life.

It didn't take them much over a couple of hours to find Rochester. The saddle and saddle bags were still there, so Frank was encouraged he would find the rest of his supplies in the cave. He still didn't have full strength in his right arm, so Bill offered to carry the saddle to the wagon. Since Frank didn't complain about the odor of the saddle, Bill didn't have the heart right then to tell him he would never be able to get the smell of the rotting flesh out of the leather. *He's struggling with the idea of losing anything, but he appears to be an eager learner. I'll teach him how to make a saddle to replace this one,* thought Bill.

Once the saddle and saddle bags were loaded into the wagon, they untied Penny and headed up the trail to find the cave. Frank felt very lucky when he saw that the branches he'd put in front of it's opening looked undisturbed, and when he discovered everything was still just as he had left it, he breathed out a sigh of relief, grateful he hadn't lost everything again. Bill helped him load the pack onto Penny. As they started back down to the wagon, Frank offered a silent prayer of thanks for the good fortune to have recovered all of his belongings. He also thanked the Lord for all Bill was teaching him and for the superb job he had done sewing him up. The scar on his face was still pretty ugly, but he knew Bill had taken special care with the stitches and it was healing well. And to have ended up on a horse ranch which belonged to kind and loving people, Frank couldn't help but recognize these as priceless tender mercies. On the way back, with his belongings intact, he realized it had been a long time since he had felt this much contentment. In spite of his concern about getting full strength back in his arm and the smell out of his saddle, Frank was feeling extremely grateful.

*****

As he healed physically, Frank noticed he was also healing emotionally. Maggie and Bill were easy people to be around, and their love for each other was reflected in the cheerful happy atmosphere of their home. Sometimes that saddened him when it reminded him of his own happy family. *I hope I can have a home like theirs and a family like the one I lost someday,* he thought. As the days passed, Frank also began to pay more attention to his surroundings. Life on the Hartman Ranch was a far cry from his lifestyle in Philadelphia, but he loved working with horses and enjoyed the physical labor required for maintaining the ranch. The Hartman's home, though simple, was well kept, but he began to notice the chairs squeaked every time they sat on them. One day he picked one up to examine the problem and saw the joints weren't as well fitted as they should be. He wished he had brought some of his woodworking tools with him. The tools Bill used to make saddles were adequate but wouldn't allow him to do the kind of finishing work he did on carriages. He would just have to make do. At first, he was going to surprise them, then he realized the surprise would be up after he fixed the first chair. Still, he wanted to try.

"Maggie, may I take one of your chairs out to the barn? I'm working on a project and it would help if I can sit down for a while." *A small lie to hide a surprise is okay, isn't it, Lord?*

"Of course, you dear boy," she said.

Frank was pleased she fell for the ruse and hoped maybe when he finished the chair and took it back, she wouldn't notice it wasn't the same.

Maggie was getting dinner ready when Frank brought the repaired chair in, so he just set it in its place. The smell of her cooking made this one of Frank's favorite times of the day. When they all sat down to eat, Maggie got a surprised look on her face and jumped up like there was a snake on her chair.

"What's the matter love?" cried Bill.

"My chair didn't squeak," she exclaimed, picking it up to inspect it.

"Will you look at that! You did this, didn't you, Frank?"

He didn't respond. The sheepish look on his face was the answer.

"Look at this, Bill. He not only fixed it, but see how nice it looks."

Bill took the chair from Maggie and turned it over.

"Why, Frank, you didn't just fix it. This is a work of art. It looks like a different chair." Both Maggie and Bill were so pleased with the repaired chair, Frank couldn't remember ever having been hugged so much.

"If you don't need me for anything else tomorrow, Bill, I can fix the other chairs."

"You bet," replied Bill, still turning Maggie's chair over and over. Fixing their chairs seemed like a small thing compared to all they had done for him, including Bill teaching him to make a saddle, but Frank was pleased to be able to use his skills to do something that made them so happy.

He stayed on with Bill and Maggie for another two months. They insisted he was more than welcome. He began to feel like one of the family. It was a healing experience. He also enjoyed getting to know and train his new horse which he named Target. Target was dark brown and had a small white spot around his right eye, so the name seemed to fit. Target also took to Penny which added to Frank's confidence about his choice.

Helping Bill with his horses was also a great experience and one he enjoyed very much. Although he was good at recognizing the qualities that made for good carriage horses, he discovered there was a lot more he needed to learn. Bill taught him how to discern their personalities and develop the skills needed in training them. He was a good teacher, and Frank was more than grateful for all he was learning. As he became confident in his newly gained knowledge, it gave him the idea that someday he would like to own a horse ranch of his own and develop a breed of top quality carriage horses. The cities on both the East and West Coasts were growing, so Frank knew there would be a demand for good well-trained horses. With the railroads expanding, Frank figured it didn't matter how far West he ended up, he could ship his horses by train to most, if not all, of the major Eastern cities. Maybe Sid Tillman would remember him.

Frank used his woodworking skills not only to fix the Hartman's chairs but he helped Bill and Maggie improve the structure of their wagon by making the sides removable, thereby making it easier to load. He mended fence and assisted Bill with reroofing their house. Since he discovered he enjoyed working with leather, after finishing his saddle, he made himself some chaps and a whip, feeling like a kid with new toys. All the while, the strength was coming back to his arm and he got so he could work a full day before his shoulder started to ache.

"If you're going to be heading West on your own, you better get yourself some survival skills," insisted Maggie. She taught him how to mend his clothes and cook over an open fire. She was a good cook and a patient teacher. Bill taught him to snare small game. Later, Frank would discover how valuable their instructions were.

By the end of the third month, his arm was close to 100 percent, so he decided it was time to move on. He wasn't sure where he wanted to end up, but he felt compelled to go further west. He hoped he had at least one good month left before winter set in.

"If you go past the Mississippi," Bill warned, "you're going to need to learn to use a gun. There's not much law out that way."

"Thanks, Bill. I'll heed your advice. I can't thank you enough for saving my life and for all the things you've taught me."

"You've more than paid us back with your help, but just pass on the kindness when you get a chance and we'll be even."

"I promise to do that," said Frank, as they shook hands.

He gave Maggie a big hug. "I'll have to go a long way to find anyone that cooks as good as you, Maggie. I feel a bit spoiled," he said, smiling.

"Yes, you are," she said, as she whacked him on the shoulder. He was aware of only a slight discomfort. That was good. He smiled inwardly.

"And you take care, Frank Madison. We're going to miss you," she said.

"I will," responded Frank. "And I'm going to miss you, too. Perhaps more than I realize since I don't really know what I'm getting myself into."

Maggie smiled at him with tears in her eyes. It hadn't gotten past her that she and Bill had filled in for the loss of his parents and that he was heading into an unknown future. *Lord, watch over him. He is a fine young man.*

4

Not Philadelphia

It was only a couple of weeks after leaving Bill and Maggie's ranch when Frank began to fully realize how valuable their lessons were. With his food supply gone and not having come across another town, he lived on rabbit, possum, and snake meat. He didn't much care for the possum, but he learned to handle rabbit and snake meat. This kind of food was a far cry from his diet in Philadelphia. *This experience is of my own making,* he reminded himself one night, as he was chewing on a tough piece of rabbit meat.

When he finally reached another town, he bought a gun, a holster, and a throwing knife. The knife Bill had given him worked for skinning animals but it was small and didn't have good balance, so he bought a knife that could not only be used for hunting but was sharp enough for various other uses. The man that sold it to him included a sharpening stone and showed him how to use it. He guaranteed it was one of the best throwing knives he could own and, if he took good care of it, it would stay sharp. The gun belt and holster were secondhand so they were already broken in. Frank thought it would make it easier to get used to wearing them. The new ones he tried on felt stiff and awkward. Walking out of the mercantile wearing his chaps and a gun belt made him doubly aware of how really changed his life was.

*****

The country he was traveling through was pleasant. The rolling hills were covered with soft green grass and there were plenty of streams with tree-covered banks. Now that he had a good supply of food again, he decided not to wait until he got to the Mississippi to learn to throw a knife and use his gun. He found a secluded spot by a river and set up camp. By continuing to snare rabbits, he was able to extend his food supply and, in spite of the cooler weather, spent a month developing his defense skills. Each night as he built his campfire, he couldn't help but thank the Lord for all that Bill and Maggie had taught him. He hoped they knew the many ways they had saved his life.

Frank was excited the day he realized he could consistently hit every target he aimed at, but sensed he was still clumsy handling the gun. Getting it in and out of the holster was slow and awkward, but he was making progress. It was taking longer to learn to use his knife successfully. He wished he had someone to give him pointers. *There must be a particular way to hold it so it stays straight instead of wobbling through the air. I'll just have to be conscious of how I grip it each time.* Although somewhat frustrated with his inability to throw a knife accurately, the exercise was good for his arm. The pain was gone, and he was sure his former strength was back. His scars were healing, but he realized they would be a permanent reminder to thank the Lord for his life. However, his changed circumstances would be a permanent reminder of the loss of his family. *At some future day, I hope a family of my own will fill that void. In the meantime, I'll stave off the heartache with concentrated effort developing my ability to live successfully in these new circumstances.* He started spending extra time throwing his knife.

When he finally felt as though he was prepared to handle himself in any situation, he packed up and started heading West again. After traveling for a week, he came to another beautiful spot by a river that offered both shelter and easy access to the water. He again set up a campsite. The further away he got from his former life the more conscious he became of his need to rely on himself for his own welfare. It had been a long time since having any contact with another human being. On this particular night, however, while gazing up at the magnificence of the star-filled sky, he became more aware that he had a habit of talking to the Lord. *It's not so much that I'm lonely,* he thought, *but that I've never been alone.* Then he realized that when talking to the Lord he had a sense that he was being listened to. It was a comforting thought.

Frank had been at this campsite several days when he was joined by a group of cowboys pushing their herd up north. He was both delighted for the company and cautious, not knowing what to expect.

"Mind if we share your spot, friend?" asked the trail boss.

"Sure," answered Frank, reassured by the feeling these were just regular people.

"You traveling alone?" the man asked, as the chuck wagon pulled into the spot where Frank was camped.

"Yes."

"That's mighty brave, young man. Which way you heading?"

"West. Are you familiar with the country out there?" inquired Frank.

"Been roaming this land for thirty years, son. Not sure I'd want to go it on my own, though."

"Name's Frank Madison," he said, offering his hand.

"Chet McFerguson. My cook's Fred Jones. You're welcome to join us for supper." Frank hoped they had something other than rabbit and hard tack.

It was a seven-man crew. Five old veterans and a couple of young men Frank guessed to be about eighteen or nineteen. They were all hot and tired, so after eating (the most delicious steak Frank had ever tasted), most of the men hit the sack. Frank noticed that one man was assigned to keep watch.

"Where are you coming from?" Frank asked Fred, as he was closing up the chuck wagon for the night.

"This cattle's from a ranch in Kentucky. We're taking them up to Chicago."

That was not the direction Frank wanted to go, so he didn't ask to tag along, but Fred looked as if he, like Chet, might have traveled the country.

"Do you know how long it will take to get to St. Louis?" inquired Frank.

"Depends on how fast you want to travel," answered Fred. "You could make it in two weeks with hard riding, but from the looks of your pack horse, I would suggest taking more time."

At that point, Frank realized what a really good pack horse Penny was. There were times when he didn't feel like stopping and had pushed her for long hours. He compared his gear to that of the cowboys and saw how much he was expecting her to carry. Of course, the cowboys had a chuck wagon, but Frank decided to reevaluate his supplies. Growing up in Philadelphia, he never had to do without anything. *I had everything I wanted. There's a difference between every-thing I want and what I actually need.* He decided to accept a new challenge. *I think I'll see how efficiently I can live. Yeah, I'm not in a hurry,* he said to himself. *And I think I've got plenty of supplies to take it slow, so I'll assess my real needs.* This new idea made him chuckle to himself. He hadn't exactly been moving that fast and he had been proud of how he had been adapting to a new lifestyle.

"What are you doing traveling alone?" asked Fred Jones.

"My family's all dead. Killed in a train wreck. I thought I'd see what life out West had to offer."

"Can you use that gun you're packing?" asked Fred.

"I think so," replied Frank. "I don't know, really. I've never had to use it."

"Show Kit what you can do in the morning. He's the one with an eagle feather in his hat. He's our best man with a six-shooter. Had to kill a couple of would-be rustlers last week. He'll be able to tell you what your survival chances are. There's some mighty rough country once you get past the Mississippi."

"So I've been told," said Frank. "Thanks for the suggestion."

The next morning, while most of the men were bathing in the river, Frank saw a man with a feather in his hat cleaning his gun. Approaching he said,

"Hi, I'm Frank Madison. Fred tells me I should check with you to gauge my chances of surviving out West. I grew up in Philadelphia and I'm not sure how far west I'm going, maybe all the way to the coast."

"You know how to use that gun?" asked Kit.

"I've spent a month teaching myself, but I have no way of judging my skills."

The man holstered his gun and said, "Walk with me."

When they were several yards away from camp, Kit pointed to a small bush about thirty feet away.

"Can you hit that?" he asked.

Frank drew his gun, took aim, and fired. He hit the bush and felt proud.

"It took you too long to aim. Do it again."

Frank drew the gun again and fired without taking any time to aim. He came kind of close this time but missed.

"Need to work on your timing, as well as your aim. How fast you get the gun out of the holster and how accurate your shot is will determine its usefulness. No sense carrying a gun if you can't use it well. You'll eat better if you can take down game on the move, and if you need to defend yourself, your gun needs to be the first one to clear your holster."

To demonstrate, Kit pulled his gun out of his holster and hit the bush square in the middle. Frank was watching, but Kit was so fast he hardly had time to see how he did it.

"I see what you mean," he said.

"Show me your draw again," instructed Kit.

Frank did. "Need to get a lot faster. Practice economizing your moves. Your fingers need to be ready and know exactly where to grab the gun as you're reaching for it. Try making the reaching and grabbing one motion."

"However, no matter how fast you are," said Kit. "If you aren't alert to danger, you're dead. Learn to hear and recognize every kind of sound. Learn to read people. There are always clues in their body language, facial expressions, and eyes that give away their intentions. The same with animals. You'll live a lot longer if you learn to pay attention. And get yourself a rifle. That six-shooter is good, but a rifle will help you get bigger game. Small game is harder to come by the further west you go, and the larger animals taste a lot better."

"I will. Thanks for the advice."

By midmorning the cowboys were gone and Frank had a lot to think about as he packed up to head for St. Louis. *I'll winter there,* he decided. *Since life out here is very different, I think I better get good at living this way or I won't last long.* A few weeks later, just as the weather was getting uncomfortably cold, he got to St Louis. His hair was long and his beard shaggy and he couldn't remember the last time he'd bathed.

5

St. Louis

He found a stable to house Target and Penny, and a boarding-house close to the edge of town so he could easily get away from the city and practice his gun skills. He noticed right away this part of town was the kind of neighborhood he would have avoided in Philadelphia. However, a lot had changed and Frank smiled inwardly over the fact that because of his appearance he fit right in. By now, he was comfortable wearing a gun and planned to get better at using it. Since the neighborhood was in a rough area, he hoped just the fact that he was wearing one would keep him safe. The next day, walking past a couple of unsavory-looking characters, he was sure wearing a gun had saved him from getting mugged. If it was useful in the city, he was sure he'd received good advice that as he moved further away from civilization, developing an ability to use his guns expertly would be essential.

He didn't need a job, but he thought he would look for one to keep from depleting his money reserve. One of the banks was look-ing for a teller. Frank got a haircut, trimmed his beard, and bought some new clothes. With his accounting background, it wasn't hard to get the job. He mentally thanked his father for sending him to school. On his first day at work, he was concerned about what would happen when he had to serve the female customers. When he was eighteen and started attending balls, his good looks became problem-atic. He'd been overwhelmed with female attention which he didn't know how to handle. It made him uneasy around girls. He wondered if he would experience that same problem and maybe lose his new job. That morning several young women came to his station but didn't give him a second look. *Maybe I like having a beard.*

Having always been an eager learner, he started acting on the advice he received from Kit. Buying a rifle took some time. He didn't know what to look for exactly, so he examined every brand and style available.

He finally decided on a Springfield. He liked its balance and simplicity. It didn't take as long to learn to use it as it did his six-shooter. The basic principles were the same.

It wasn't long before he also started getting better at paying attention to people and the sounds around him. As he practiced watching the people in the bank—the way they moved and their facial expressions while they were talking—he learned to pick out the gist of conversations even if they were across the room. He listened to the traffic outside and even got familiar with the sounds of individual carriages that passed on a regular schedule every day. He could definitely distinguish the sound of the milk wagon. However, it surprised him that in all the years he spent making carriages he had never noticed that each one had its own unique sound.

One day Frank became aware that during these months of honing his awareness skills, he'd developed the ability to read lips. That skill let him in on the secret the bank practiced to prevent being wiped out by a robbery. On a slow afternoon, while watching the bank manager, Mr. Crawford, and his assistant talking, he perceived their conversation was about the bank's secret vaults. *Good strategy,* he thought.

A few weeks later, he took notice of several men who came into the bank. Two opened accounts. One applied for a loan. Normal bank stuff, but something about them just didn't sit right with Frank. Several days later, they were back. Frank watched the men talking and realized they were planning a robbery. He passed on his suspicion to Mr. Crawford. The next day the attempted robbery was foiled and the men were taken into custody. Frank received the customary reward.

As the months passed, Frank continued to work on his preparations to acquire the skills he would need to travel further West. When he went out on weekends into the unsettled country around the city, he began to rely solely on his ability to obtain his own food and shelter. He was determined to be successful at this new way of life, so even in the cold weather, he spent the whole weekend in the wilderness. He could feel his confidence growing. He improved his ability to get by on essentials, eliminating things that could prove a burden. Once he learned to live on what he could carry in his saddlebags, he reluctantly sold Penny. He felt good about the progress he was making in other areas, also, developing his listening skills which he practiced both in the city and out in the wilderness, and improving his ability to use his gun and rifle and his knife. Frank felt as if his draw had gotten pretty fast. However, with only a remembrance of how fast Kit had been, he was only guessing.

Target was grazing nearby. Frank learned that after spending all week in a corral, Target liked the feeling of freedom, so Frank trained him to not stray too far when he left him untethered. Because Target was smart, he caught on fast. Besides, they were becoming the partners Bill said they needed to be and valued being together. The short periods of time Frank spent with him during the week weren't enough for either of them, so they both cherished the time they spent together.

On weekends away from the city while gazing at the night sky, Frank's mind always drifted to memories of his family. This usually caused feelings of loneliness. One spring night, however, he noticed something different. The sadness wasn't as oppressive, so he started contemplating what it was about his family that had made them so happy. *We never questioned father's love for mother or their love for us. Mother was our champion. She was always so supportive and happy about our achievements. I was so grateful she taught me to dance. It helped me feel confident going to my first ball, until I was swarmed by all those girls.* Tears still rolled down his cheek when he thought of Sophie. *She was so pretty. I bet she would have been swamped by all the young gentleman, but she never even got to buy her first ball gown and will never know the happiness of having her own family. Someday I'll have to think about getting married. I hope I can find a girl like mother. She was as skilled at her responsibilities as father was at his. Father had a kind heart. I need to remember his example. And he was a man of integrity.* People trusted our carriages to be of the highest quality. His thoughts drifted back to the teachings of his father. *He taught me his skills with patience and never got upset with my mistakes. When I started making parts for actual carriages, he was so insistent they fit perfectly. "Our success is not a result of our carriages looking good when they are new, but because they maintain their appearance as they age," he would say. "The movement of a carriage will eventually cause the joints to come loose. When they are perfectly fitted, that eventuality is delayed. Our reputation is a result of people knowing our carriage will maintain their good looks longer." How many times did he tell me that?* Frank wondered if his father's demand for perfection was what had driven him to work so hard to develop the skills Kit and the Hartmans said he would need to survive traveling across untamed country. He also wondered if there was a connection between his progress in using guns and the natural dexterity he had always possessed. *Maybe I was cut out to be a Westerner,* he thought.

A few weekends later, after once again leading Target through both deep and shallow water and over a variety of different terrain, Frank was satisfied with their success. "We did well today, didn't we, boy? Maybe we're ready to move on. What do you think, Target? Are we ready for some new experiences?" Target stuck his muzzle into Frank's chest. He took that as a yes.

*****

A month later, near the end of April, after quitting his job at the bank, Frank was surprised at how much money he had saved. Added to the money from his estate, his dream to buy land and horses was becoming more and more a real possibility. Now all he needed to do was find the perfect place. Before leaving St Louis, he set up an account in a bank that had a branch in Denver and several other

Western towns. Knowing it would be foolish to carry even bank notes with him, he decided to only take twenty dollars in cash. There wouldn't be much need for money until he found a place to settle. He'd been informed that there was little in the way of civilization until he reached the Rocky Mountains, but Frank was confident now in his ability to live off the land.

6

The Test

A few weeks after leaving St Louis, Frank camped with another group of cowboys from Texas driving a herd to Chicago. This time he didn't feel like such a green horn. However, the true test came one evening a week after that. The country was dry and desolate. He spent hours looking for at least a puddle left over from last week's rain. The sun was getting low in the sky, and just as he was thinking maybe he should push on during the night, Target started acting up. "Do you smell water, ol' boy?" Frank let go of the reins and gave the horse his head. As a result, they found a good size watering hole. "You have a good nose, Target, my friend. You may have just saved us." Frank took off Target's saddle and rubbed him down and was just finishing eating his cooked rice and a strip of hard tack when two men rode up to his campsite.

"Hey, mister," they asked, "You willing to share your water?" He didn't get a good feeling about the men, but agreed to let them linger.

"I'm Tim, and this here is Rex," Tim said by way of introduction.

"Frank," he responded, but didn't shake hands. "Where are you boys headed?"

"New Mexico Territory. We just got off a cattle drive."

"Well, I've got some rice left from my dinner. You can help yourselves."

"Rice," responded Rex. "You don't look like a Coolie?"

"No," said Frank, wincing at the slur. "I just like a variety in my diet and besides rice cooks faster than beans."

"Where are you from?" asked Tim. "You don't sound like you're from around here."

"Philadelphia."

"Where the heck's that?" he responded.

"On the East Coast."

Shrugging, the men got out their eating utensils and finished off Frank's rice. Frank sat with them for a while but there was little conversation. He was annoyed they hadn't taken care of their horses. As they sat around the fire, Frank had a feeling of uneasiness and avoided staring at the flames. After adding some more sticks, he stood up and turned to get his bedroll. That's when he heard the creaking of leather against steel. Frank drew his gun and put a bullet in the dirt between the two men before Tim's gun cleared his holster.

"You have two choices," he told the startled men.

"Leave your gun belts on the ground and ride out or get buried here."

Grudgingly, they took off their gun belts. Frank walked them over to their horses.

"Ease those rifles out of their scabbards and drop them on the ground."

"You expect us to ride out without any guns?" whined Tim.

"Like I said, leave your guns in the dirt and ride out or get buried here."

"You're a hard man," said Rex.

"This is a hard country," responded Frank.

"After I'm gone, you can come back and get your guns. But if I see either of you again, I'll know you've chosen to make this your gravesite."

Grumbling, the two men mounted their horses. Frank heard one of them say, "He doesn't look like a gunslinger, but did you ever see anyone draw that fast?"

Frank smiled, feeling grateful that he now had an idea of his skill and was thankful again for Kit's advice, without which this might well have been his gravesite. That night, when he talked to the Lord, he thought about the Hartmans and Kit and expressed gratitude for putting those people in his path, knowing how essential they had been to his survival. The quiet night also brought thoughts of his family again, along with a reflective sadness, but he slept well. Target would warn him of any danger.

7

The Journey's End

Three weeks later, Frank arrived at a mining town called Wylerton. He wasn't sure what made him decide to stay for a while. It was a rather small rough-looking town, but the surrounding countryside was magnificent.

He felt comfortable in Wylerton, and it wasn't long before he began to develop some affection for both the town and its people. Other than the Hartmans, he couldn't remember ever knowing people as friendly and easy to be around as the mercantile owners Isaac and Beth Ann Perkins. He struck up an almost instant friendship with the blacksmith, Hank Wilder. Since Hank had also lost his family and both were skilled tradesmen, they had many things in common. Because of his easygoing nature and propensity for kindness, it didn't take Frank long to acquire quite a few friends. For some reason he took an interest in old Elvira Wyler. He couldn't imagine any woman having lived such a hard life, yet she was as cheerful as anyone. Frank decided to play the Good Samaritan and keep her woodpile stocked. He lived in the hotel but built a little shack outside of town on the side of the mountain. After cutting and splitting the wood from several dead trees, he filled up his shed, but only replaced the wood Elvira used each day thinking she wouldn't notice what he was doing.

Another reason Frank found Wylerton appealing was the land available around the town. There was a good size river, rolling grassland, small buttes, and high mountains. The perfect place to establish a horse ranch. His dream began to seem a real possibility. In the meantime, the Barnes Hotel was clean and well run, so he decided to take his time and explore the area. Once he got to know it better, he could decide if this was the right place to settle.

*****

Frank had plenty of money, but when he discovered the Jackson Mine was looking for an accountant to manage the payroll and silver deposits, he felt inclined to seek the job. The Jackson brothers were delighted to find someone with Frank's education and experience and hired him on the spot. Having always been curious, Frank soon took interest in learning about the operation of the mine. He sat down with Willie Barton one day for dinner.

"Willie, how did you learn to be a miner?"

"I used to be a cowboy. One winter I got caught in a blizzard heading back to Texas. I found a rock outcropping to ride out the worst of the storm, but it was still snowing the next day and I couldn't get my bearings, so I took the path of least resistance and ended up here in Wylerton. That was about fifteen years ago. There wasn't much here then—the mercantile, Hank's blacksmith, a few mine worker shacks, and the big house the Wylers built. A couple of months later, when Mr. Wyler found out I was broke, he offered me a job. I didn't know a thing about mining, but he was real good to teach me and the pay was so much better than I could ever make cowboying, I just stayed on."

"Would you be willing to teach me? I've been hired to handle the payroll, but I'd like to learn about mining." It wasn't long after that that Willie and Frank became good friends.

Originally hired because of his accounting experience, the Jackson brothers soon learned the broad variety of abilities Frank possessed, including his capacity to get along well with people and his skill with a gun. They were impressed with his interest in learning how to mine.

One of the brothers was planning to go back to Denver to manage some pressing responsibilities at their silver refinery, but when they came to see Frank's integrity was without question, they decided to both return to Denver and leave the entire operation of the mine in his hands. His talent for understanding people helped him discover which men worked well together. So after he took on the responsibilities as the manager, he organized some new crews. As a result, the mine was doing well and so was the town. When John Tucker discovered a silver deposit a mile away from Wylerton, some of the men left to work there, but Frank regrouped his crews and was able to maintain almost the same level of production. With two silver mines in the area, the town continued to grow.

8

Old Lady Wyler

The old woman sat on the bench in front of the hotel waiting for the arrival of the afternoon stage, thankful it was a relatively warm day for February. She didn't get out much these days. After twenty years of roaming the country looking for gold, when she and her husband Clarence found a rich vein of silver, they decided to count it good. Being tired of living in a tent, they built a house and put down roots. When they took their silver to Denver, they hired workers who in turn built houses. Eventually, they encouraged a blacksmith and his family and some young shopkeepers from Georgia to settle in the area. Thus, the beginnings of the little town named Wylerton, after its founders. For the next fifteen years, the community worked together helping add to their town as needs arose. First, a church, then the school. Eventually, a bank and a cafe. Clarence and Elvira made sure each new family that came to the area was cared for, encouraging a spirit of friendship and peace. Their only disappointment was that they never had children of their own.

After Clarence's death, Elvira sold the mine to the Jackson brothers—good honest men who she knew would treat the workers as well as they had. She sold their large house to a bank in Denver (which was turned into their Wylerton branch) and moved into a small house next to the mercantile. The Perkins, who owned the mercantile, had been some of the earliest settlers and were taking good care of her. She lacked for nothing.

Most of the town's children thought Elvira Wyler was a witch. True, her wiry gray hair was unruly and made the old woman look scary, but she wasn't a witch. She did, however, have an uncanny gift for discernment. The children judged her by her looks, but many of the grownups suspected she was the town's fairy godmother since money or other things always seemed to be provided with a surprisingly accurate correlation to needs when they arose.

Elvira's presence at the stage stop was not without reason on this February afternoon. Last year, when a tall well-built young man moved into town, he reminded Elvira of her Clarence. He was thoughtful, kind, and cheerful and was quickly well liked by many of the townspeople. She began to keep an eye on him. The first time she heard him talking to Beth Ann Perkins, she knew he was a gentleman. Not only for his Eastern accent but because of the courteous manner of his address. He had dark blue eyes that sparkled like moonlight on a lake, and she suspected he was handsome. His beard, an effort to cover something on his face, a birth-mark or scar perhaps. Shortly after his arrival, Elvira's woodpile was miraculously restocked each morning. The Perkins feigned ignorance, so one day she took a long afternoon nap and sat by her back door all night. Somehow, she wasn't surprised to discover the Good Samaritan was Frank Madison, the tall newcomer. She invited him to tea, and not long after her first invitation, she invited him to join her for dinner. This was the beginning of their regular visits once or twice a week. It made her think, for this young man to take an interest in an old woman shows he has a good heart.

Being a romantic, Elvira considered the young women in town. None were a match for her Frank. When the Johnsons took over the management of the bank last month, she considered their daughter Claire. But Claire, although intelligent and pretty, was a quiet mild young lady. *No, my Frank needs someone with spirit.* Hence, her presence that afternoon waiting for the arrival of the stagecoach. She had a feeling what she was hoping for was going to arrive that day.

The minute the tall handsome gentleman stepped out of the stagecoach with his daughter and teenage son, she knew why she had come. The dismay on the beautiful girl's face didn't surprise her.

45

Elvira could tell from the style of their clothes that they were from the East and that her little town was a disappointment, if not a shock, to the young woman. However, as she watched, the girl's body language was enough to let Elvira know that Frank Madison's match had arrived. The young lady squared her shoulders and gave her brother a squeeze, took a deep breath and smiled at her father. Those little gestures told Elvira the girl had tenacity and spirit. They showed a determination in the girl that said she would eventually triumph over what Elvira suspected was a big change in her circumstances. She pulled her coat snug around her shoulders and headed for home. Two days, later she joined her beloved Clarence in the place we call paradise.

9

Grace

W hen she was fifteen, Grace was surprised by her mother's insistence that, along with her academic and social training, she learn to cook and participate in other household chores. She had always envisioned after her elementary schooling she would go to a finishing school. But instead Grace discovered her mother was going to instruct her at home. Thinking it beneath her to work in the kitchen and clean house, etc., she couldn't understand why she needed to learn such things. *Isn't that why we have a cook and a maid?* She thought. *And I can't understand why I need to learn to sew when we have plenty of money. I can buy anything I want.* The idea seemed so ludicrous. Besides, her friend and neighbor Caroline was at finishing school. Being kept home meant they hardly ever saw each other. However, it wasn't long before Grace caught the vision of being knowledgeable about both domestic skills and those of being a lady. The experience turned out to be much more fun than she imagined and she was glad she hadn't been sent away to school.

As the wife of a bank owner, Charlotte Saulsby moved in the highest social circles, but, as they worked together on her education, Grace came to realize that, in addition to her intelligence, her mother also possessed both humility and wisdom. Under her tutelage, Grace discovered that her mother was not only outstanding as a woman of refinement, she was capable and independent in many areas and it was her idea that a woman should be well-rounded and skilled in every way. Her mother didn't care for the overly sophisticated training popular in finishing schools and Grace soon gained respect for all that she was learning. *My mother is an amazingly capable person,* she thought.

Grace found some of the chores tedious, but she discovered she liked to cook. They gave Cook an extra day off so Grace could have actual experiences in the kitchen. She found it fascinating to put different spices and herbs together and discover the results. She started experimenting with them, creating her own seasoning mixes. It wasn't long before the pantry started filling up with jars of different herb and spice concoctions. She loved learning which herbs and spices worked together to enhance the flavor of meats and which combinations enriched the flavor of vegetables. One of her discoveries was a spice mixture that was wonderful on potatoes and another that added flavor to pot roast.

"Grace," her father said after finishing a roast beef and potato dinner she had prepared, "I don't think I've ever had a more tasty meal. You certainly know how to turn ordinary food into a feast."

"Thank you, Father. But you should really thank Mother. I'm so glad you didn't send me away to finishing school. I'm sure she has let me be much more creative than any school I would have attended."

*****

By the time her mother unexpectedly became pregnant again and was ordered to bed, Grace was a very polished young lady. She easily took over the responsibilities of managing the house and kept things running smoothly. This would prove to be a much needed heritage two years later when she became the only woman of the house.

But there was one thing Grace still murmured about.

"Why can't girls go to college?" she complained one day to her mother.

"I know it isn't fair," explained Charlotte. "Someday maybe they will be allowed to but, in the meantime, Grace, you have a good mind and we will buy you any book you are interested in or you can avail yourself of whatever the library has to offer and educate yourself."

That idea sat well with Grace and she was determined to make a go of it. Caroline Barlow, her friend and neighbor, had been sent to a finishing school, but had come home in less than a year. She'd hated it and had refused to go back. Therefore, Grace was hopeful she would be interested and willing to join her in this endeavor. She went to talk to Caroline that very afternoon and found her in the parlor reading a book—a good sign.

"Caroline, have you ever wished you could go to college?"

"Are you kidding?" she exclaimed. "My brother is so full of himself since he started going to college, I can hardly stand him. He is always bragging about what he is learning. 'Poor Caroline,' he says. 'Too bad you're a girl. Girls are so disadvantaged.' Can you believe that? We used to be so close. I can hardly believe how arrogant he has become. And that finishing school my parents sent me to—it was awful. Even if I grow up to be a complete dunce, I refuse to go back. You're so lucky your mother kept you home. But never mind that, I think going to college would be grand. Why are you asking?"

"I have this really great idea, Caroline," she said. "Well, actually, it was my mother's idea, but still. How would you like it if we worked together to educate ourselves? We could get books from the library, and my parents have agreed to buy any other books we need. If we work together, it should be fun. What do you think?"

"I would love that!" said Caroline. "Sometimes I get so bored reading by myself. Let's keep it a secret, though. I don't want my brother Ralph to find out. He would pester me to death. If I get a chance to show him up every once in a while, though, I'm going to take it," responded Caroline.

That very day Grace and Caroline when to the library. They decided to start with ancient history since it was a favorite subject for both. As they were sitting in the library, they discussed how they were going to proceed. They decided each would start reading a different book and write a test as they finished each chapter.

"At the end of the first week, we will exchange books. At the end of the second week, we'll take each other's tests," said Grace.

"That should work," responded Caroline.

Since both were determined to do well, they were quite competitive. But as friends, they learned to study well together and help each other succeed. It took three months to get through their history studies, but they fell into a successful pattern of studying together, and then spent as much time on the other subjects as their interest and desired mastery level dictated. They spent a couple of months studying mathematics and botany simply because those would be required subjects if they were actually attending a real college, even though the one they often found boring and the other sometimes difficult, but for Grace fascinating.

If she and Caroline hadn't gotten so caught up in current history, they probably could have mastered this subject in a few months. But they spent so much time discussing each issue and consulting with other people, it took longer than they planned. They loved sharing their studies with Charlotte, who never failed to be impressed, and since Caroline's mother was more interested in social clubs and playing bridge, Caroline started spending a lot of time at the Saulsbys'. That proved a blessing since the current events sessions often became heated and Charlotte was always able to put out the fire.

Caroline told Grace she loved it when she was able to hold her own against her brother's bragging on more than one occasion. They didn't share these activities with any of their other friends knowing that not all girls wanted to be educated in the same way as men. But for Grace and Caroline, it turned out to be more fun than they even imagined. It changed their friendship and made them much like sisters. After nine months, feeling happy with their progress, Grace and Caroline wished they could get their hands on some real college tests to check their knowledge, but they were encouraged enough that they decided to continue their studies the following year.

*****

During and after his wife's pregnancy, Allen Saulsby was pleased with the woman his daughter was becoming. She was efficient at managing the house, the dinner conversations were vibrant and challenging. Although she had been mindful of her brother Charles, he was surprised at how willing she was to help with her new little brother James after he was born.

"It was a stroke of inspiration for you to be Grace's teacher rather than sending her away," he told his wife. "So many of the young girls that come into the bank are so spoiled and self-centered. I sure hope our sons will find girls like Grace when they get old enough to marry."

"Grace is not only going to make some man a wonderful wife, she already has the heart of a mother. I hope she finds a man worthy of her," responded Charlotte.

"So do I," said Allen, as he kissed his wife.

*****

The night of the debutante ball, when Grace came down the stairs, even her thirteen-year-old brother Charles was impressed. Her creamy silk and white lace dress with gold ribbon trim was a perfect complement to her dark auburn hair and delicate complexion. Her mother tied cream-colored ribbons in her hair but left ample curls hanging down in the back. Grace looked the epitome of her name. Allen hadn't thought any woman was as beautiful as his wife, but he recognized Grace had become her equal. With his wife Charlotte in a dark blue silk gown that set off her still slim elegant figure in spite of their three children, he was sure he was escorting the two most attractive women in Richmond to the ball that night. On the way to the ball, Allen thought, *I wonder if Grace even realizes how uniquely beautiful she is. She is always so driven to improve her mind and her other abilities. Since she admires her mother so much, perhaps she simply counts beauty as part of being a lady.*

Caroline was a very pretty girl with bouncy blonde curls and a personality to match. In her pink lace dress, she was the very picture of a Southern belle. Grace, on the other hand, could not be considered cute. Because of her height and her rich dark hair, her beauty would have to be described as elegant and regal. When Grace and Caroline arrived at the ball, they became the center of attention, at first, because of their appearance, but it didn't take long for the young men to become aware of their ability to carry on intelligent and interesting conversations, making them both a novelty and very popular.

Since their private educational activities were secret, it was fun to keep everyone guessing about their wealth of knowledge. Grace was not as outgoing as Caroline, but many of the young gentlemen were attracted to her stately deportment and, found it fun to challenge her on a variety of subjects because her detailed thoughtful responses were so atypical and often humorous. She and Caroline never lacked for either dance or conversation partners. What added to Grace's attraction was a beauty that reached clear to her soul. Everything about her reflected the refinement of a true lady—the way she spoke, the way she moved, the way she regarded others. As she and Caroline entered into society after the ball, they became the two most popular debutantes in Richmond. At age eighteen, Grace was a delightful young lady, not only because of her appearance but she also had an inner beauty that made people comfortable in her company. Because of these qualities her success as a debutante was impressive. Without being aware of it, Grace had reached a personal goal to be just like her mother.

However, just as Grace was becoming one of the most sought-after young ladies in Richmond, her mother, father, and baby brother James contracted scarlet fever. Her father recovered, but when her mother and brother James passed away, the family was devastated. As a result, Grace was snatched out of that wonderful sociality that was the life of Richmond's upper class. Losing her mother was a crushing blow to Grace. She and her mother had become so close during the past few years, happiness was a daily expectation Grace had taken for granted. Educating herself had been so much fun partly because of her mother's support and interest. Losing her almost destroyed Grace's desire to go on. The black mourning clothes she wore were an outward reflection of her spirit. Her grieving was profound. She withdrew from society. The dark cloud that filled her spirit caused her to lose enthusiasm for life. In spite of frequent attempts to keep up their studies, Caroline eventually gave up. However, she did everything she could to maintain their friendship.

For a long time after assuming her mother's place in the household, Grace went through the motions like someone in a daze. Then one day she found Charlie sitting in the corner of his room, sobbing.

"Charlie," Grace said, throwing herself on the floor next to her brother. "What's wrong?"

"No one loves me anymore," he sobbed.

"But Charlie, Dad and I both love you." Grace suddenly realized she was not alone in her grieving. She had been so centered on her own grief she hadn't noticed how Charlie had been affected by their mother's and James's deaths. Her heart went out to him and she began to see she needed to pay more attention to his needs.

"I think we are all grieving over the loss of Mom and little James and have forgotten to appreciate each other. I'm so sorry, Charlie. I love you very much, and I'll be more careful from now on to make sure you know it," she said, giving her brother a big hug. After this, she also began to recognize the change that had taken place in her father and became more aware of his suffering. Thinking about these things caused her to turn her focus to them, and she realized this was helping with her own healing.

Gradually, after two years of filling the void of her mother's absence, Grace started to be willing to make a reentry into society. It didn't take long for her to attract the attention of one Stuart Sullivan. He was away at school when she made her first debut, so Grace hadn't met him at that time. He was handsome and charming. His family, wealthy plantation owners, moved in the highest social circles. Not long after he started calling on Grace, her father decided to pull up stakes and move west.

*****

Grace knew something was going on when she saw the correspondence coming from Denver.

"Father, why are you getting letters from Denver?" she inquired.

"I'm just looking into some investment opportunities," was all her father would tell her. Little did she realize at the time her father's investment opportunities would land her in a Western mining town in the middle of nowhere.

Allen Saulsby's original idea was to buy into a bank in Denver, but when that didn't work out, he started looking at other options. The Denver bank had a branch in a mining town further west. He applied for the job as manager of that bank. But because communication was slow, it was filled while his application was in transit. However, Mr. Johnson, who was hired as the new bank manager, informed Allen of an opportunity to purchase the town's land and title company, explaining that the McNeals, who owned the company, wanted to move back to Chicago and were looking for someone to purchase their business. The deal included a large two-story house. Mr. Saulsby decided this was the kind of change he was looking for, so he sold his bank and his house, packed up his two children, and moved out to the mining town of Wylerton. Neither the town nor the country was anything like Virginia.

10

Charlie

Charles Saulsby, a happy energetic teenager, was thrilled with the move to Wylerton. What sixteen-year-old wouldn't be? The opportunity and freedom to explore a wide open unsettled country, it was a teenager's paradise, especially since Charlie as already an excellent horseman.

When he was growing up, because he was tall, at the age of ten he was enrolled in riding classes. Before the end of the year, he had nearly mastered the jumping course and excelled in both riding skills and grooming. It couldn't have been more fortunate that he made fast friends in Wylerton with Rich Davies, a boy whose family owned a cattle ranch and several horses.

Because Charles was smart, he should have been an exceptional student, but he had too much energy to sit for long periods of time studying. He did the required work because he knew what was expected, not because he enjoyed being in school. As a result the teachers in Richmond mistakenly classified him as having average intelligence. His parents, however, knew better and recognized his need for activity. They spent a good deal of effort to engage both his energy and his mind. During the summers, his mother had put him to work planting and weeding their flower beds which kept him occupied for at least an hour a day before he would run off to play with friends. Charlie actually developed a fondness for the work because he was encouraged to learn the names and characteristics of both the plants and the weeds. When his father discovered he had an aptitude for numbers, he starting teaching him about finances and the operation of the bank. The summer he turned twelve, Mr. Saulsby started taking him to the bank once a week. It didn't take Charlie long to learn how to balance accounts. Knowing she could trust him to be responsible, his mother put his excess energy to work by sending him into town to the store almost every day. She knew the grocer, Mr. Patterson, would make sure he got everything on the list and that Charlie would come home with the groceries and the right change.

When they moved to Wylerton and Charlie complained about having to attend school, his father was not surprised, thinking it the same old song and dance.

"Dad, I'm the only boy my age in the whole school."

This was a new argument, but Allen had no intention of forgoing his son's education.

"Charles, you know very well your education will continue until you are eighteen."

Charlie knew his father wouldn't relent. In Richmond, school was a given for boys his age. The young men in Wylerton stopped attending school at age sixteen.

Not knowing what educational opportunities would be available, Mr. Saulsby, wanting to ensure his son's continued education, brought all the books Charles would need if he'd stayed to attend school in Richmond—two trunks of books. The hope being that if schooling wasn't available, Charles would let Grace tutor him, but when he balked at that, he was required to attend the one-room school in town. Charlie knew his options. He didn't like either one.

The schoolmaster, Mr. Jenkins, was a good teacher and did his best to challenge Charles. He even used him to assist with the younger students, but Charles felt awkward since he was the only person in the school his age. What made it even harder, Rich Davies loved having Charlie come over and ride with him. This made having to attend school even more of an embarrassment. Other than that, Charles Saulsby loved living in Wylerton.

11

Adjusting

O n the other hand, when Grace first stepped off the stagecoach and surveyed her surroundings, the small rough-looking Western town seemed like a nightmare to her. The cheerfulness and the enthusiasm for life that she was beginning to regain after her mother's death disappeared; her throat constricted as her eyes welled up with tears. She realized the life she knew was gone. Not only did the town look bleak, so did her future. She took a deep breath and squared her shoulders, deciding in that moment, for her father and brother's sake, she would endure. She gave her father a weak smile, and her brother a hug. The only small consolation was the charming two-story house that her father had purchased along with the title company. Located just outside of town off the main road, it was painted a soft sunny yellow. There was a covered porch along the whole front of the house, with a bench swing on it. The other porch outside of the kitchen door was large enough to hold a covered wood bin. Because the cold weather was something she wasn't used to, Grace became grateful not to have to trudge out to the woodpile every time she needed to bring wood into the house. The large piece of land around the house was covered with prairie grass and had a nice fence around it which reminded her of home. But her favorite thing was the full-grown cottonwood tree in the backyard.

"Thank goodness. At least we have a tree," sighed Grace.

With the exception of the trees on the mountains, it was the only tree anywhere near the town. Because it was February, the tree was leafless, but Grace could picture its beauty in the summer. It gave her an idea. She pictured herself sitting in its shade. *As a substitute for the refinement of the sociality I enjoyed in Richmond, I will escape reality by reading. We have two trunks full of books. I can continue my education by reading every one of them,* she decided.

*****

It wasn't long after they arrived that Grace realized that their clothes, especially hers and Charlie's, were totally unfit for their new circumstances. After getting settled in, she went to the mercantile and bought yards of fabric, then spent her first month sewing. By the end of March, most of her dresses were altered and she had also made herself some simple cotton skirts and blouses like the ones the women in town wore. Many of Charlie's shirts were okay, but she had to make him new pants that were less formal and more suited to the colder climate and new lifestyle. She even made Charlie and her father wool coats. Sewing wool was quite different from the fabrics she was used to and proved to be a challenge. She had to buy a few extra yards of material because of mistakes, but after having to replace several ruined pieces and a lot of restitching, she was satisfied with the results. She still had two ball gowns and several other dresses that would have been considered rather plain in Richmond, but even though she thought they were too dressy for Wylerton, she just couldn't bring herself to dismantle them. *Even if I never get to wear them again, I'm going to keep them as a remembrance of my former life.*

At first, the snow was fascinating, but Grace struggled getting used to the cold. During February and March, she mostly avoided leaving the house. Because the title company was in town and her father went to work every day, she made him a list of the items they needed allowing her to only leave the house to attend church. Winter, the dirt roads, the colorless wooden buildings were so different from the life she had known. By avoiding the town and concentrating on her sewing and reading, Grace alleviated some of the discouragement she felt. But even after two months, she was still feeling like a displaced person. With everything unpacked, the sewing finished, and an efficient housekeeping routine worked out, she had plenty of time to read. But, even with this one bright spot, she was still struggling to accept her new life in Wylerton. She prayed for help every night but often found herself in a black mood when she thought about her future.

There were times during the winter months she felt gratitude for two things—her mother's wisdom in teaching her homemaking skills and the time she and Caroline spent studying. *I wondered if, without that, I would have been as interested in the books we brought with us.* She thought back to how she complained when her mother insisted she learn domestic skills. "In case of a rainy day," her mother had said. Of course, neither ever imagined this kind of rainy day. So whenever she was able to throw off her dark mood, Grace felt grateful that her mother hadn't given in to her whining.

*****

Although glad not to be living in town, for a while, the quietness kept Grace awake at nights. She had grown up with the constant hum of the city and it scared her. She should have counted it a blessing not to be too isolated or live in a small shabby house in town. However, on this particular sunny April day, since she was feeling discouraged about her current circumstances and the need to make a rare trip into town, her mood didn't match the sunny weather. For some reason, in spite of the beautiful April morning and the mountains alive with wildflowers, Grace's mood was one of discontent. There was still a bit of chill in the air which made her think of the cold snowy days that lingered into March. And, the still unpredictable nature of the weather, made her wonder if it would ever really get warm. Today as she often did, she pondered what kind of future lay ahead for her. When she kept busy, which hadn't been hard while setting up the house and sewing, she could sometimes feel resigned about her change of circumstances. Today, however, she was in a dark mood and the bread dough was taking the brunt of her discontent. *I understand father wanting to leave Richmond after the fever took Mother and James. A different way of life, that would help him get over his guilt for surviving. But why here?* Then she thought, *I can do this. Charlie loves it here, and I think Father is enjoying his new challenge. My life will not be what I was expecting, but please, Lord, help me to at least help Father and Charlie be happy.*

The town is just plain ugly, she thought, as she finished kneading the dough. (She had always appreciated the beautiful tree-lined streets in Richmond and couldn't understand why, with plenty of trees in the mountains, anyone would build an entire town and not plant a single tree.) "However," she said out loud to convince herself, "It is a lovely day and we are getting low on sugar and cinnamon and all this fresh air is definitely agreeing with Charlie because he has grown out of the pants I made him two months ago." Thinking she had sewed her fingers to the bones, she was put out about having to make Charlie a new pair of pants. *Perhaps I should count my blessings and be glad the cold weather is almost gone. I hope.*

Never having experienced spring in Wylerton, she wasn't sure what to expect. Because she had to acknowledge the good weather and felt a need to get out of the house, Grace was trying to feel resigned to the trip into town. She realized, however, she had taken her frustrations out on the bread dough and hoped it would still rise. After balling it up and putting it in a bowl, she covered it with a cloth, washed her hands, and cleaned up the kitchen. As she got ready to go, she thought about the Johnsons. The Johnsons were well-traveled and had lived in both New York and Chicago. They had been very kind when they first got to Wylerton, helping them get settled into the house and several times inviting them to dinner. They lived in a stylishly decorated apartment over the bank. Their daughter Claire was Grace's age, and they quickly became friends. She was a pretty soft-spoken girl, and Grace was more than glad to have a friend. When they first met, Grace was puzzled as to why on earth they moved here from Chicago. So one Sunday after church, she asked Claire about it.

"My mother has asthma. The smoky air in Chicago was hard on her. My father wanted to go somewhere where the air was clean and dry. So when he learned the bank in Denver needed a new manager for their branch here, he went there in person to apply for the job.

Even during the winter, Mother has been so much better since we moved here."

Although her father had also wanted the bank job, Grace was glad things had worked out the way they did. She reflected on more than one occasion that if it weren't for Claire and her letters from Caroline, she might have gone crazy. *Maybe, I'll stop in and visit Claire,* she thought.

She put a shawl around her shoulders, grabbed her purse (and in spite of her resolve to make the most of things), slammed the door as she left the house. The thought of visiting Claire hadn't been quite enough to lighten her spirits.

I miss Caroline, she thought as she started a reluctant stroll toward town. *The letters we exchange are fine but nothing like being together.* She could tell Caroline was leaving out information she thought would upset her.

Subconsciously, her pace grew slower the nearer she got to town as she contemplated the way her life had changed. She realized she missed riding. It had been one of her favorite pastimes. The riding trails and parks in Richmond were some of the best in Virginia. There were no riding trails in Wylerton, and since it only took a few minutes to walk to town, her father hadn't done anything about setting up a stable. *Perhaps I should have insisted on getting a horse to replace Bessey. But what is the point? There is no place to ride around here. I am grateful for the house, however.* Having been built by a family from Chicago, it wasn't just a one-story building made of rough lumber. *Now that I'm used to the quiet, I'm glad we don't live right in town on a dusty street.*

In keeping with her black mood, Grace continued to ponder her current circumstances. The Jackson Silver Mine and the new Turner Mine were productive and new people are buying land on a regular basis, so the title company turned out to be a good investment. *We have plenty of money. However, having money in Wylerton doesn't offer the same advantages it did in Richmond. In Richmond, I associated with well-educated and culturally refined people and had a wardrobe of beautiful dresses. I wonder if Caroline is enjoying wearing those ball gowns I gave her. With her blonde hair, they probably look better on her, anyway. Stuart surely has some lucky new girl dangling on his arm. Maybe Caroline. I'm sure she is more popular than ever. I'll probably never get to attend another ball. I'll bet there's at least one new dance everyone is crazy about. I'm going to end up an old maid and never find the man of my dreams.*

Grace thought about her mother who she loved and admired and remembered when she had become aware of her mother's place in society. Peeking around the wall at the top of the steps when she was ten, she watched the elegantly dressed ladies and gentlemen as they entered the house. Her parents were having a formal dinner party for all of the bank executives. She had been in awe of the glamor. As she watched, she began to see her mother as a person who had an important standing in society. Charlotte Saulsby wore an elegant but simple burgundy silk dress and not nearly as much jewelry as the other women. However, Grace thought she looked the most magnificent. She watched her mother interact with their guests, making them feel welcome and, from the reaction of the people with whom she was talking, her conversation must have been entertaining. Grace remembered deciding that night she wanted to grow up to be just like her mother, (Still unaware that through her mother's tutelage she had achieved this goal).

Since she was going into town to buy cinnamon, she worried about what she would do when her seasoning mixes ran out. *I'm glad Father let me bring them with me.* Then her thoughts turned to how glad she was that she had learned to sew; the time she spent sewing for her father and Charlie, altering her clothes, and creating new things out of the old turned out to be a blessing. *It was a good way to spend my time during the winter months.* However, none of these thoughts and reflections did much to brighten her spirits. She used to hum a favorite song when she was having the blues, but there was no music in her today. When she got to town, she was still frowning.

12

Frank Finds Grace

He saw the young woman up the street as he came out of the bank. His attention was drawn to her when he noticed the graceful way she walked. She was tall for a girl, but there was nothing gangly about the way she moved. He felt compelled to watch her. Although she was wearing a simple brown cotton skirt and a cream-colored cotton blouse, her movements were elegant and her trim well-shaped figure brought back the memory of the girl in Richmond. Occasionally, his thoughts still lingered on the strange way just the touch of her skirt had affected him and how the way she moved was like watching a ballet dancer. He often wished there had been an opportunity to make her acquaintance and regretted not having seen her face. Watching this girl awakened that memory and he stood there feeling drawn to her. When she stopped at the curb to determine if it was safe to cross the street, she turned her face his way. His breath caught. It was that new girl he'd seen in church.

Frank always sat on the back row in church with Willie Barton and Hank Wilder. They left as soon as the sermon was over to avoid the social chitchat. In spite of his beard, the scar on his jaw made him shy away from casual interaction with people. Ever since the experience at his first ball when he was surprisingly overwhelmed by girls wanting to dance with him, he felt insecure in the company of women, but having a scarred face added to his insecurity. This girl hadn't been hard to miss because she was both tall and beautiful.

After that, he always paused a minute to look at her before leaving. At first, he wondered if it was just because of her beautiful face, but decided it was because he felt somehow drawn to her and could feel she radiated an inner beauty. Although he also perceived in her a sense of melancholy, his very soul responded to her and he had been puzzled by this reaction. It wasn't as if she was the only attractive woman he had ever seen. However, in spite of being instantly drawn to her, he had never made any attempt to make her acquaintance.

Now, as he stared at her, he was again taken in by her beauty. She was regal-looking in spite of her frown. Today, however, as he watched her cross the street, he was aware that it wasn't just the beauty of her face that was pulling him toward her, and causing him to have a desire to get to know her. It was a need connected to something in the very core of his being.

Maybe because she was alone or because watching her walk stirred that old memory, whatever it was, he took a deep breath and squared his shoulders, determined to make her acquaintance.

The dirt on the path she took into town was hard packed, but the heavily used streets in town made them much muddier. Grace was grumbling to herself that she had to cross the muddy street to get to the mercantile. *Why don't they put some cobblestones on these streets?* she thought, as she gathered up her skirt to keep the hem from getting dirty. When she entered the mercantile and Mrs. Perkins greeted her with a cheerful "Hello," Grace was reminded that there were people here that she liked. She had gotten acquainted with the Perkins at church. Mr. and Mrs. Perkins were from Georgia and had brought their Southern hospitality with them. Grace couldn't help but smile and return her greeting.

"What can I do for you today, sweet pea?" said Mrs. Perkins.

"I need a pound of sugar and a tin of cinnamon, thank you, Mrs. Perkins, and I'm going to look at your fabric. My brother is growing out of his new pants already."

"He's a right strapping handsome boy, that's for sure, and probably growing like a weed," replied Mrs. Perkins.

"That he is," replied Grace.

She was looking at the fabrics when someone came in the mercantile. She didn't turn around at first to look at who it was but she knew it was a man. She could feel his presence. It seemed to dominate the store.

"Hello, there, Frank," said Mrs. Perkins cheerfully. "What can we do for you today?"

"I'm in need of a new pair of gloves, Mrs. Perkins," he said. It being the only excuse he could think of for being in the store.

His voice was warm and rich with a slight Northern accent. Grace turned her head to look at him and saw he was looking at her. She was surprised. His appearance didn't seem to match his rich smooth voice. He was quite shaggy-looking with rather long wavy dark brown hair and a full beard. However, his stormy blue eyes seemed to penetrate her soul. She couldn't pull her gaze away from him, as he smiled at her. It made her blush.

"Miss," he said, touching the brim of his hat and nodding.

Without acknowledging his greeting, she quickly turned back to the pile of fabric and grabbed a bolt of light tan cotton.

Even though she knew he had walked to the other end of the store to get gloves, Grace could feel his presence. For some reason, she felt as if she wanted to know him. She stole a glance. He was tall, perhaps a little taller than her father who was six feet. He was wearing a gun. She wondered if he was one of Sheriff Singleton's deputies. His shoulders were broad but not big like the blacksmith's. His cotton shirt was loose fitting, but because his sleeves were rolled up to his elbows, Grace could see he had strong arms. However, she had seen a number of strong well-built men in Wylerton, so why then did this man's presence seem to fill the whole store? Why did she feel as if a connection was being made between them? She didn't recall ever seeing him before. Was he new in town?

"I'll take three yards, Mrs. Perkins," said Grace, laying the fabric on the counter.

"Good to see you, Frank," greeted Mr. Perkins, as he came from the back room. "You needin' another pair of gloves? I didn't realize paperwork was so hard on a man's hands," he teased.

"You know I still work with the men in the mine twice a week," replied Frank, smiling. His voice full of merriment.

So he's a mine worker.

"How are things going now that you lost some men to that new Tucker Mine?"

"It looks like we are going to have to hire some part-time help until we can bring in more men. I'm going to be putting up notices tomorrow."

"If I was a bit younger, I could use a little boost to our income. Beth Ann here wants one of those new stoves with a warming oven, but my old back wouldn't last a day working in the mine."

"Yes, those are very nice stoves. I'm sure your business will do well as new families move into the area, Mr. Perkins. And the men I hire are bound to spend some of their money here in your store."

Although mesmerized by the sound of his voice, Grace was trying hard not to think of the man, and didn't notice his movement. When she turned to go, after Mrs. Perkins had wrapped up her things and because she was looking at the floor, she ran smack into him. Her insides froze. She was so aware of the warmth and strength of his body, time stopped. When she finally came to her senses, she didn't know if hours or seconds had passed.

"Oh, I'm so sorry," she said and hurried around him without looking into those piercing dark blue eyes. But his touch, it affected every nerve in her body. Distressed by the experience, she hurried out of the store and headed for home, forgetting completely her plan to visit Claire.

What I felt bumping into that man wasn't a normal reaction. Why did I have such an unusual response to touching him? she thought as she almost ran home.

Frank was also puzzled by his reaction to the girl's touch. *I haven't felt anything like that—well since that girl's skirt brushed against me in Richmond,* he thought. He went to the window and watched her hurrying down the street, still impressed by her grace. She must live in that yellow house just outside of town.

He always took special notice of Grace in church, but today he knew there was something different about their meeting. Up close, he realized that her beauty was a result of the strong but refined bone structure of her face and that her features were a perfection of harmony. Everything about her face was a pleasing balance to her dark auburn hair. However, in addition to her beauty, there was something just plain different about this girl. She had stared at him, it was true, but it was not a blank stare. Because he had learned to read people, he could tell this was not a bit of fluff in a beautiful package. He encountered many beautiful women while growing up in Philadelphia and while living in St. Louis, but not one of them had affected him like this one did today. *With the exception of that girl in Richmond. The girl in Richmond! Could this be her?* The touch of both girls had taken his breath away.

Frank was definitely going to get to know this woman. There was something special about her. Since her touch made his heart jump, he knew that somehow she was important to him.

"Mrs. Perkins, who was that young lady that just left?" he asked.

"Why, that's Grace Saulsby. Her father owns the land and title company."

Grace, hmmm, how appropriate. "I see," he said aloud.

"They moved here from Richmond, Virginia, but I get the feeling Grace is not taking to the change very well. Except for attending church, she seldom comes into town, and the few times she does, she's always frowning," explained Mrs. Perkins.

"She perks up after a cheerful greeting, but I think she's missing Richmond." *She's from Richmond? She's from Richmond!*

"Yes, this place is a big change from there," responded Frank, hoping Mrs. Perkins couldn't detect the quiver in his voice.

"Oh, are you familiar with Richmond then?" asked Mr. Perkins.

"Yes, I've been there a few times," he answered, as he was still watching Grace hurry home. "I was born and raised in Philadelphia. My family owned a carriage shop. Occasionally, I would go to Richmond to deliver carriages and get some special hardware."

"What brought you out here from Philadelphia?"

"My family was killed in a train derailment. I didn't have the heart after that to carry on the business alone, so I sold my estate and decided to make a new life for myself, as you might say."

"I'm so sorry about your family," said Mrs. Perkins. "I can't imagine how hard that was."

"Yes," replied Frank. "But I'm glad I didn't stay in Philadelphia. I've enjoyed a lot of new experiences coming West." *One of them being running into Grace Saulsby.* "Well, thanks for the gloves. I better get back to work."

Grace Saulsby is from Richmond! It couldn't possibly be the same girl! Could it?

13

Reflections

Grace had never walked home as fast as she did after leaving the mercantile. She stamped her foot twice when she took off her shawl and got ready to bake the bread. *How dare that scruffy-looking man affect me so. It felt like a spider, attaching silken threads to me. I can still feel the effect of his touch and the way he looked at me.* Distracted, she almost burnt the bread and dinner wasn't up to snuff, either, but she was glad neither her father nor Charlie complained.

After dinner, as Grace was washing the dishes, she was still thinking of those dark blue eyes that seemed to pierce into even the private corners of her mind. *As if he perceived the very depths of my soul.* She stomped her foot again.

"Are you all right, Grace?" her dad called from the parlor.

"Yes, Father, I was just killing a spider," she lied.

She wished she had really stepped on a spider and smashed it to bits. Maybe that would alleviate her puzzlement about those silken threads that had sprung out from her heart and made her feel attached to that man. But the frustration remained in spite of her stomping. She simply could not stop thinking about her strange reaction to that shaggy-looking man.

*****

Charlie had taken off right after dinner. Now that the weather was getting warmer, he would run over to the Davies Ranch to ride with his new friend Rich. The boys would ride most every night until almost dark. Rich was also teaching Charlie about cattle ranching. Grace was glad Charlie had made such good friends with one of the local boys.

There were several young ladies in town about Grace's age that she was getting to know. She especially liked Claire Johnson and was glad for their friendship. Minnie Stewart and Priscilla Jones were pretty girls, but Grace found them rather empty-headed and a bit silly. All they wanted to talk about were the Clarke brothers. She'd met the Clarke family at church. They ran a lumber mill. The older boy, Roger, worked with his father at the mill, but the younger son, Jeff, worked in the mine. They were the best-looking bachelors in the town and they knew it. Grace wasn't impressed. However, Grace wasn't impressed with anything about this place. Upon this reflection, she scolded herself because she should be grateful that the McNeals, from whom they bought their house, had some taste and had built a very nice house. She had to admit that it was charming, and as she thought about it, she was again glad she didn't live in one of the houses in town that were right on the street. *Where's my gratitude?* she thought. *However do those people keep their houses clean with so many horses and wagons going by them all day? I can't imagine. At least we are off the main road and have a grass yard.* She sat down in the parlor and picked up the Bible. Maybe she could find something in the scriptures that would help her to reconcile her current circumstances and take her mind off the man with the stormy blue eyes.

"Are you settling in any better, daughter?" asked her father.

"I'm okay, Father," answered Grace, knowing her father's concern.

"With two silver mines in the area, Wylerton won't be a small town forever, you know, and many of the new folks will be from back East, like us and the Perkins. Things are bound to change."

"Yes, I know," agreed Grace, but didn't share her father's optimism.

That night, however, Grace reflected on her strange physical reaction to the shaggy-looking man in the mercantile. *Why was I so affected by his touch? His very presence? Stuart was handsome and charming, but I never had that kind of reaction to him. Maybe the bleakness of this place and my future is making me desperate. If we get acquainted, he will probably turn out to be as disappointing as the Clarke brothers. What's to become of me? I'll just have to concentrate on Father and Charlie and forget about myself.* Grace went to bed praying she could keep this resolve.

"Hear my cry, O God; attend unto my prayer. From the end of the earth will I cry unto thee, when my heart is overwhelmed: lead me to the rock that is higher than I" (Psalm 61:1–2).

She pulled her comforter up around her chin, sighed, and tried to imagine she was floating on clouds.

14

Experiences and Changes

Frank would forever regret the day he had to put down his beloved horse. The experience was still weighing heavily on his spirit. He'd been so caught up staking out a very good meadow that he'd lost track of time. "We need to hand out the payroll in the morning," he explained to Target as he was urging him on. The sun was already below the horizon and darkness was setting in fast when Target stepped in a snow-covered gopher hole. Frank was thrown to the ground. The fall knocked the wind out of him. By the time he came to his senses, he saw Target writhing in pain. He was immediately seized with both fear and regret. Because there was still so much snow, he should have known better than to be pushing to get home when it was so dark. He checked Target's leg, hoping beyond hope the break wasn't too severe and there would be some way to save his beloved horse. But both the shin and knee bones were broken, there was no hope of repair. Even knowing Target was in pain, it took Frank a minute to put him down. Afterward, he sat on the ground resting his head on Target's neck, sobbing. He thought of all the times he might have been lying dead if not for this horse. Along with this present grief, all the memories of losing his family flooded his mind. *Why didn't I just decide to camp for the night?* he wondered, wishing he could go back in time. *A little delay in handing out the payroll wouldn't have made that much difference. I didn't have a choice in losing my family, but this is all my fault.* "Oh Target, my dear friend,

I'm so sorry." Glad to have been alone where he wasn't ashamed to cry, Frank finally drifted off to sleep, the approaching darkness in keeping with the darkness filling his soul.

Sometime during the night, he woke to behold the star-filled sky. A sense of loneliness filled his heart, but again there was something else—a feeling, though faint, that someone was sharing his sorrow. He had a sense of being loved. This was not the first time he'd had this feeling. While these feelings were stirring in his heart, his thoughts turned to the good hardworking men that would be receiving their pay in the morning. Along with a sorrow he'd only experienced once before after losing his family came a feeling of responsibility. He removed Target's saddle and hid it under a nearby rock outcropping, then, picking up his rifle and canteen, he set out on foot. "I'll come back after distributing the payroll, Target. I'm not going to just leave you here for the buzzards." If he walked at a fast steady pace, Frank knew he could make it back to town by morning. As he hurried through the night, the guilt of losing Target weighed heavily on him. Memories flooded his mind of the numerous times he owed his life to his faithful intelligent horse. He may have been grateful he was only a few miles from town, but in spite of the faint sense of being loved, his grief was too profound to think of his own comfort.

The next morning after distributing the payroll, Frank went to the blacksmith shop. "Hank, I had to put my horse down last night."

"Not Target!"

"Yes, I was pushing to get home before dark. He broke his leg stepping in a gopher hole. I left him and my saddle out on the prairie. I'm going to borrow a wagon from Joe and I was wondering if you could go with me. I want to cremate him. I can't just leave him out there for the buzzards."

"Oh, Frank, I'm so sorry. What a loss. Target was one of the finest horses I've ever seen, and you two shared a rare bond," responded Hank, as he put his hand on Frank's shoulder. "I'll be glad to go with you. Let me just finish shoeing Luke's horse and I'll be ready."

An hour later, Frank came back in a wagon loaded with a bundle of straw and some scrap lumber. He and Hank didn't talk much as they traveled. Hank could tell Frank was suffering. He remembered the heavy sorrow he himself felt when he lost his family and knew Frank had also lost family and experienced great suffering, but losing his horse, especially when he considered it his fault, would be hard on any man, and Hank was aware that because of Frank's caring nature he would be doubly hurting. His heart ached for his friend.

After the cremation, Hank offered to drive the wagon back to town. Everything about Frank's body language indicated he was feeling pretty low. *I hope he will be able to pull out of this,* thought Hank. *I don't think I've ever seen anyone so down.*

After several weeks, Frank still couldn't foresee a time when he would ever feel happy or care about life again, until the day he ran into Grace Saulsby—actually, when she ran into him—and his spirit was rejuvenated. Not just rejuvenated but awakened to desires he had almost given up on. Out of some pull he couldn't resist, he had followed her into the mercantile and something happened there. He wasn't sure why, but this girl infused new life into him. He realized after meeting her he not only had a great desire to get to know her but actually felt a renewed interest to pursue his dream to own land and raise horses. He made a decision that he would make Wylerton his permanent residence. A few days later, with a heart still feeling the loss of Target, Frank walked into the title company, ready to buy the land he and Target had surveyed.

*****

Without knowing why, after the day she bought the fabric for Charlie's new pants, Grace began to have better feelings about living in Wylerton. It didn't occur to her that it had anything to do with the man in the mercantile. When she thought about him, she was puzzled and disturbed by her reaction to him but didn't connect him to her changing attitude. *Maybe it is the coming of spring,* she thought. The cottonwood tree was leafing out, starting to shade the ground around it, and she was looking forward to the time when she could sit in its shade and read. In the meantime, she started enjoying sitting on the porch in the late mornings feeling the warmth of the sun. She was sure it was ruining her complexion. *But what does that matter now?* she mused on a particular warm sunny day while she dozed over a book of poetry. Her mind wandered to her life in Richmond. Although her memories of there still caused a sadness to fill her heart, she realized it wasn't as heavy as it had been during the cold winter. *Winter, there is something I wonder if I'll ever get used to.*

Then she thought about her current situation. *This time, after so much experience sewing men's clothing, making Charlie's pants has become routine and this last pair didn't give me grief like they did when I first made the attempt.* She chuckled at the thought. *Sewing men's clothes was not something mother taught me. Of course, neither of us guessed how much my circumstances would change.* In the past, such thoughts would have produced tears but today only reflective contemplation. She thought about how she still loved experimenting with her spices, especially on the new kind of meat called venison that they had eaten several times.

She looked at the book she was holding. *These books we brought are quite engaging. I wonder if Charlie will ever let me teach him.* She missed having someone to share ideas with. *Well, if I'm going to be successful about helping Father and Charlie be happy, I'd better learn to accept my unfortunate circumstances with a little more grace.* She chuckled at the pun.

15

Beginnings

Grace got all the housework done early so she could go into town and talk to Mr. Jenkins about Charlie's progress. It was a lovely sunny day, and she remembered her resolve to focus on Charlie and his education. With the brightness of the day, she was encouraged this spring weather might just be the answer to avoiding her disappointment with the shabbiness of the town and the dreariness of her future. As she neared the town hall—just another wooden building only distinguishable by the sign over the door that said *Town Hall*—she saw a line of men waiting to go in. Sunday on their way to church, she had seen the posted notices. The Jackson Mine was looking for temporary part-time help. She was wondering why anyone would want to work in a dark hole in the ground when she spotted her brother Charles. Grace knew if Charlie was planning to sign up there was no way she would be able to talk him out of it, so she picked up her skirt and ran as fast as she could to her father's office.

"Father!" she yelled, very unceremoniously, as she burst through the door. "Charlie is in line waiting to sign up to work in the mine!"

Only after this frantic declaration did she notice her father was talking to a customer. Not just any customer. The shaggy man with the dark blue eyes.

"Oh, I beg your pardon," she said breathlessly. "I didn't see you."

Frank only nodded and smiled. An amazing smile that made his eyes twinkle. Grace felt one of those silken threads reach out from her heart to him.

"Now, Grace, calm down," said her father. "You know Charlie is too young to work in the mine."

"What if he lies about his age? You know he looks older than sixteen." Suddenly perceiving her behavior was very unladylike, she said, "I beg your pardon, sir. I realize I've been quite rude. I'm sorry for interrupting, but if my brother signs up to work in the mine, it might cause a bit of a stir to unsign him."

"I think I can be of some assistance there," said Frank, smiling at her agitation. The warmth of his voice enveloped Grace's heart. "I'm the foreman of the mine and those men are lined up waiting for me. No one under the age of eighteen is allowed to work in the mine, so when your brother gets to my desk, I'll make sure I question him about his age."

"Do you know Charles?" she asked. "What if he doesn't give his real name?"

"Is his hair the same color as yours?" he asked.

"Pretty much," she replied.

"Then I'm sure I'll recognize him," he said, smiling. Again, the effect of his smile wrapped another silken thread around Grace's heart.

"Thank you," replied Grace, blushing. *The man is insufferable,* she thought as she turned and exited the office as quickly as she had entered. *Why does he have such an effect on me?* She stamped her foot. Frank was watching and smiled.

"My daughter Grace. You'll have to forgive her. When my wife and youngest son died from Scarlet Fever, Grace had to take on her mother's responsibilities. She has been a mother to Charles for almost four years now. I hope you can appreciate that she may seem overly protective. I wish she could enjoy more of the activities befitting a young lady her age."

"If I may ask, how old is your daughter, Mr. Saulsby?"

"Twenty-two. Grace has missed much of what should have been some of the most carefree years of her life."

"I understand you are from Richmond. May I ask why you left?"

"There was more than one reason, I suppose. After losing my wife and my infant son, so much reminded me of them. I just felt I needed to get away."

I know that feeling, thought Frank.

"But also, last year I needed to get Grace away from an unacceptable suitor. She was flattered by the young man's interest in her. He belonged to one of the wealthiest families in Richmond. He was very charming, but it was an attachment I couldn't accept. I don't think Grace was in love with him, but I could see he thought her a fine feather in his cap."

Yes, she would be, reflected Frank. *His loss, my good fortune.*

"Anyway," continued Mr. Saulsby. "I felt a need get myself and my family away from there. The change has been good for Charlie and me, but Grace is having a hard time adjusting. I hope I haven't made a mistake."

"I'm sure things will work out. The people here are friendly good folks. Wylerton is a growing town. It won't be like it is now forever," encouraged Frank.

"I hope you're right," said Allen as he was finishing up the paperwork for Frank's land purchase.

Grace simply could not understand how anyone who looked like that man could be affecting her so. She didn't even know his name. First, she chided herself for being judgmental. Then she got angry. *Why am I even giving him a second thought?* She stamped her foot again hoping to rid herself of even thinking about him. It didn't help this time any more than it had the other times. He seemed to have planted himself in her mind, and every time she saw him, he seemed to draw her to him. She would simply have to avoid him. *However, if he does keep Charlie from signing up to work in the mine, I would be a rather petty person not to feel some gratitude toward him.* She stamped her foot again as she made her way to the schoolhouse to inquire about Charlie's progress.

*****

Perhaps because he was young and inexperienced, Charles signed his own name on the job application. Frank smiled when he saw the signature, even though he had spotted the boy before he got to the desk. It was quite obvious he was Grace's brother. Because of his youth, he was almost as pretty as his sister.

"How old are you, young man?" Frank inquired.

"Eighteen, sir," Charlie lied, wishing he had a bit more facial hair.

"Well, Charles Saulsby, I was just in your father's office and I happen to know you are only sixteen. If you are still interested, you'll have to come back in a few years when you really are eighteen."

"That's not fair," cried Charlie. "I can work just as hard as anyone in this line."

"Perhaps it's not fair," replied Frank. "But it's mine policy. Sorry, son."

Charlie sulked away, cursing himself for not thinking to sign a false name. He just had to get out of going to school. It was just too embarrassing. He had grown five inches in the last three months so he was taller than Mr. Jenkins. *Maybe I'm going to have to let Grace be my tutor after all.* He was in such a state when he got home he didn't even feel like going over to Rich's. It was going to be so mortifying to give in and ask Grace to teach him. He could hear her banging around in the kitchen and could tell she was in a rage about something, so he decided to go straight up to his room and sulk for a while.

By dinnertime, Charlie had pondered his educational choice and come to terms about asking to be taught by his sister. When he blurted out how he had tried to sign up to work in the mine and how the mine foreman had known he was only sixteen, Grace and her father exchanged knowing smiles. But when he confessed to wanting to have Grace tutor him, they were shocked but overjoyed.

"Your sister was an excellent student," said his father. "You know she and Caroline Barlow studied together enough that it was equal to a year of college. I'm sure you will enjoy having her teach you."

"I suppose so," confessed Charlie. "It's got to be less embarrassing than going to that school. Do you realize I'm taller than Mr. Jenkins? Even the little kids are starting to laugh at me."

"Oh, Charlie, why did you wait so long to make this decision?" cried Grace.

"I don't know. It just seems so humiliating to have you be my mom and my teacher."

"Charles, that's nothing but pride and it's not very becoming," snapped his father. "Grace has done an excellent job filling in for your mother, who was also her teacher. Moreover, your sister has worked hard to educate herself. You would do well to be as dedicated about education as she was. That attitude shows me you are not as grown up as you think you are."

"I guess," replied Charles, realizing his father was most likely right.

Grace was glad her father didn't seem to remember her whining when her mother first undertook teaching her. *I can understand how Charlie feels. However, having mother be my teacher turned out to be such a blessing. I hope Charlie and I can have a similar experience.*

"Father, what is the name of that man who was in your office today? He has something to do with the mine. I should thank him for not letting Charlie work there."

"Yes, he's the foreman and manager of the Jackson Mine. His name is Frank Madison."

When lying in bed that night, Grace regretted learning Frank's name. Adding a name seemed to make it harder to dismiss his existence.

Whatever am I going to do? Out of sight, out of mind. I hope that old cliché really works.

*****

It wasn't hard to keep her resolve to avoid Frank Madison. Between taking on the responsibility to teach Charlie and the almost constant rain, it had been two weeks since she'd left the house. Charles, on the other hand, discovered that not only was Grace a good teacher, but they worked out a study schedule that suited him much better than spending five hours cooped up in a schoolhouse. She let him take afternoon breaks which consisted of helping around the house and working in the yard whenever the rain let up for a little while. Grace expressed an interest in having a garden, so Charlie decided to watch the movement of the sun and calculate where they should put it. He also started testing the soil to discover its composition. Once he decided the best place for a garden, they started working together to clear out the grass and weeds. Charlie explained it was easier when the soil was damp. Grace wasn't sure what she was going to use the garden for, but the thought of running out of her herbal mixes was worrying her. She was grateful to have her brother around more and was glad he had some experience with gardening. Some of the seasoning mixes she'd brought with her were almost gone. *Maybe I could learn to grow my own.* She noticed when Charlie could get outside he enjoyed the physical labor of yard work. *Mother taught him to weed and plant flowers to keep him busy, but he actually enjoys it. With his help, maybe we will be able to create a successful garden.*

In addition to these activities, Charlie was looking forward to being able to hang out more with his friend Rich. Also, since Grace was able to choose subject matter that catered to his interests, he was becoming much more engaged in learning.

It was turning out to be a beneficial arrangement for both of them.

*****

One Thursday afternoon, the rain let up and they made real progress on clearing their garden plot. But two days later the rain was back. Grace was staring out the window wondering how they were ever going to get to church since they owned neither a horse nor a buggy. Her poor father had been braving the weather for two weeks in order to get to work, Shank's mare being his only transportation. Her mood was as dreary as the weather. Charlie, however, was surprisingly very focused on a book about ancient history.

"Grace, how is it that a civilization as advanced as Rome could fall apart like it did?"

After some reflection, Grace replied, "Remember when you wanted to sign up to work in the mine? What was your motivation?"

"I guess I was trying to get out of going to school."

"If you had succeeded, think about how that would have affected your life."

"Well, I would have probably cut short my education," he answered.

"And that would have altered your future quite a bit, don't you think?"

"Yes, I can see that."

"Then, also, let's suppose you did go to work in the mine. What are some other possible consequences it might have caused?"

"If there was an accident, I could have been killed."

"Or injured," prompted Grace. "And how would either of those circumstances affected Dad and me?"

"I suppose cutting my education short would have limited my choices and, if I died, for you it would be like how much our life changed when we lost Mom and James."

"Exactly! You see, Charlie, the circumstances we face and the choices we make don't just affect us personally, but all the people around us. To illustrate this concept, I'll give you a new assignment. See if you can discover how the choices that the people and/or the government of ancient Rome made that changed their circumstances and lead to their downfall. However, I want you to be aware that you are reading second hand information. The history we read in books is really only someone's opinion about what happened. Nevertheless, it will be a good assignment to help you learn to analyze information and understand consequences."

Grace was good at keeping house, but for someone with a mind as active as hers, it was not altogether satisfying. Teaching Charlie was being a blessing. She loved the challenge and often felt more content. She enjoyed the time she had spent reading, but now with purpose and direction, her reading became more focused as she endeavored to stay ahead of Charlie's studies. Once the premise of a given subject was established, Grace let Charles be self-directed. As a result, he settled into his study routine with more enthusiasm allowing Grace time to once again pursue her own education. They started having some wonderfully stimulating conversations. Nothing had lifted Grace's spirits as much since she and Caroline had studied together. She often thought about Caroline, wondering how she was doing. It had been several months since she had received a letter. But unlike a few weeks ago, this didn't plunge her into a black mood.

One day she remembered that when Charlie was attending school Mr. Jenkins was having him assist the other students. *He might be missing the help since Charlie is no longer there.* She was intrigued with the idea of offering her services for a few hours each day and decided the next sunny day she would go talk to him. A sunny day. Grace was beginning to notice how long it had been since she had seen one of those. They'd had to forgo church again last Sunday not only because of the constant rain but also the soaked ground. She wondered why people like her father, who had to get about in this weather which turned the streets into mud puddles, didn't insist on doing something about them. *Maybe Father likes cleaning off his muddy boots every night.*

On Tuesday, the rain finally let up, but Grace waited a day to see if the good weather would hold and give the ground time to dry out a bit before she decided to take a chance and go into town. The next morning when the weather was still good after getting Charlie's assignments organized for the day, Grace set out to talk to Mr. Jenkins.

*****

The older children were focused on their schoolwork when she entered the schoolhouse but she could quickly see that Mr. Jenkins was overwhelmed trying to help several of the younger students of various ages and levels of learning. He looked up with a weary expression on his face which he quickly replaced with a smile.

"May I help you?" he said.

"Well, you see, Mr. Jenkins, I'm here to see if I can help you. I've come to see if you would be interested in having an assistant for a few hours a day now that my brother is no longer attending."

"Young lady, that's about as welcome an offer as asking a thirsty man if he wants water. When can you start?"

"I'm sure if you tell me what needs to be done I could get started right now."

"Bless you, Miss Saulsby. You may have just saved my sanity. These are wonderful children but there is just not enough of me to go around."

Mr. Jenkins showed Grace the math problems the eight-year-olds were working on. She quickly perceived what she could do to help them by pairing them up so two children could work together much the same way she and Caroline had helped each other. When the lunch break came, she had made good progress learning the students' names and found it rewarding to work with a small group of five or six children. Mr. Jenkins thanked her profusely, and Grace said she was looking forward to coming back the next day.

She walked up and down the sidewalk several times looking for a dry place to cross the road. *It must have rained again while I was in the schoolhouse, this road is a muddy mess.* She couldn't see a dry spot anywhere. Frank had been watching her pace up and down the sidewalk. She had been standing in the same spot for several minutes trying to convince herself she was just going to have to face the fact that she had to muddy her boots and most likely her skirt, so didn't hear Frank walk up behind her.

"Have you lost something?" he asked.

"Oh, for heaven's sake, you startled me," she replied, not perceiving at first who had spoken to her.

"I saw you pacing up and down the sidewalk and thought maybe you were looking for something."

"Yes," she said, blushing and trying to avoid looking at him after realizing who it was. "I'm looking for a dry place to cross the road. I'm loathe to muddy my boots, but it looks as if I have no choice."

"I think I can help with that," Frank said, as he scooped Grace up in his arms and stepped off the sidewalk.

"Sir, put me down this instant," she cried. "Your behavior is quite improper."

"Miss Saulsby, I'm standing in the middle of the muddy road. Are you sure you want me to put you down?"

"Well, no," Grace admitted. "But this is no way for a gentleman to behave."

"On the contrary, I'm rescuing a maiden in distress. That's very gentlemanly, I think. Don't you?"

"Oh, very well." Grace had to admit to herself she didn't want to be put down in the road and was glad her boots and skirt would not be ruined. But in the back of her mind she was aware of a feeling of pleasure and the silk threads that seemed to attach her to him.

"At your service, miss," Frank said, as he set her down on the other side of the street.

She was surprised at feeling abandoned. "Thank you, sir," she replied, not very graciously.

"The name is Frank, and you're welcome, Miss Saulsby," he said, as he favored her with his knowing smile. Grace stamped her foot and marched off in a huff, confused by the pull of those fairy threads which were attaching her to this man every time they came into contact. In an effort to dispel her confused feelings, she concentrated on getting the rest of the way home without getting too muddy. *If I stay on the grass, maybe I can make it home without too much trouble.* She picked her skirt up a little bit, carefully watching where she stepped.

Frank had to smile as he watched her walk away, making an effort to avoid the mud. *I don't think she is even aware how well she fits her name. Even her concern about propriety is charming. She felt so good in my arms, I wonder what it is going to take to get to know her better.* Aware that his appearance was less than desirable, he thought about shaving his beard, but that would reveal the scar on his jaw and might prove a bigger detriment. *I'll be patient, even though getting to know her is not an option for me. I even wonder if getting her to like me is. Somehow she feels a part of me.*

Grace stamped her foot at least three times while she was fixing dinner that night. Her father smiled to himself as he was reading the Denver newspaper that came on the stage once a week.

"Are we having a problem with spiders?" he called from the parlor.

"No, it's just that odious man who was in your office the other day. That mine foreman."

"Oh, you mean Frank Madison?"

"Yes. Do you know what he did this afternoon?"

Her father had seen the whole thing as he was leaving Betty Packer's Cafe, but he wasn't about to spoil her fun.

"He had the nerve to pick me up and carry me across the street. I was so mortified. I can't imagine what people will think."

"They might think he was helping you avoid the mud," her father ventured.

"Yes, but to be carried in the arms of a complete stranger."

"Now, Grace, you know Mr. Madison is not exactly a complete stranger."

"But still," Grace replied, stamping her foot again.

That night, after organizing Charlie's assignments for the next day, she was lying in bed, thinking about being in Frank Madison's arms. She could still feel his strength as he carried her across the street as if she weighed nothing. *Even though he is a mine worker, he smelled clean. No, he smelled really good.* She was also disturbed by the fact that she felt comfortable and safe in his arms and reflected how abandoned she'd felt when he put her down. She pondered the strange fact that with each encounter she felt more and more connected to him. *Since avoiding him might prove impractical, perhaps I should change tactics and get to know him better. He does seem like a gentleman so I don't think there is any danger in furthering his acquaintance. Yes, I think I will endeavor to get to know him better. If* familiarity breeds contempt, *perhaps that will cure my strange attraction to him.*

The next morning Grace got to the schoolhouse a little early so she could get organized before the children arrived, secretly hoping she would see Frank Madison on the way. "Good morning, Mr. Jenkins. How may I help you this morning?"

"Bless you for coming early. Your students are going to be working on subtraction. If you could find twelve problems in the textbook for them to write on their slates, that should get them started."

A few minutes later, the Gilbert children came in. Grace liked the two Gilbert children. Ruth was a quiet reflective girl that liked to draw and Johnny was a happy little boy that had a cheerful attitude about everything. However, this morning Johnny was crying.

"He fell and cut his finger," explained his sister.

"Let's take a look at that," responded Grace, as she reached for the little boy's hand.

"Well, Mr. Gilbert," she said squatting down to look into his little tear-stained face. "The first thing we need to do is use some soap and water to get your hand clean."

"Is it going to hurt?" he asked.

"Well, it might," responded Grace. "It's a good thing you're brave!"

Grace smiled as she saw his eyes widen and his shoulders square. She was glad the medical book was one she had already studied and knew it was important to clean the wound.

"Mr. Jenkins, I hope you have some medical supplies. Johnny has a cut finger."

"Yes, in the bottom drawer of my desk," he answered as he was shuffling through the writing assignments for the older children.

After washing his hand and neatly tying the bandage on Johnny's finger, Grace smiled to herself as she watched him proudly showing it to the other children who were just arriving, explaining how he didn't cry at all. Grace pondered how protective and caring Ruth was of her little brother. *I wish I had developed that kind of caring nature sooner.* Then she remembered feeling that way toward James. She wondered if Charlie resented her for the months she'd ignored him after their mother died. *I'm glad I came to offer help to Mr. Jenkins. There is a good deal of satisfaction in working with children, and I'm also very much enjoying the challenge of teaching Charles. I wonder if I should become a teacher.* This thought caused a familiar but unwanted gray cloud to form in Grace's mind. *I used to have a clear picture of what my future would be. Married to a handsome successful man. Living in a beautiful big house with a wonderful kind nanny to help me with the children. Now I have none of that to look forward to. Being a teacher would be okay, but will I be an old maid? Who is there here that I would ever want to marry?* An image of Frank Madison materialized. Grace was shocked. *Wasn't the idea to free myself of curiosity about him? Why is it being so hard to rid myself of any kind of interest in him?* She stomped her foot and shook her head. It did nothing to get Mr. Madison out of her mind or the gray cloud that was developing there. Luckily, it didn't last long. The children had arrived and she was quickly engaged in their studies.

16

Getting Acquainted

Frank began seeing Grace each day as she walked to the schoolhouse. He figured she must be helping Mr. Jenkins. It pleased him. Seeing her every morning was like a cool breeze on a hot summer night. Refreshing. He was aware that Charles was no longer attending school, and knowing the Saulsbys were from Richmond's upper class, he surmised they would not have abandoned the boy's education and wondered how they were attending to it. *That Miss Saulsby is interested in being of service to Mr. Jenkins is especially kind. Her brother had most likely been a valuable assistance in spite of being a student.* He reflected on an image of Grace mothering an energetic teenager and chuckled to himself at the memory of her bursting into her father's office all excited about Charlie wanting to sign up to work in the mine.

After their several personal encounters, Frank knew his attachment to Grace was growing and watching her walk to the schoolhouse was the highlight of his day, and added to his desire to know her better. *I wonder what I can do to further our acquaintance.*

Late Friday morning on her way home from the schoolhouse, Grace ran into Frank Madison carrying a beautiful armchair out of Hank Wilder's blacksmith shop.

"My, what a fine piece of furniture, Mr. Madison. Did Mr. Wilder make that?" she inquired.

89

"Thank you, Miss Saulsby. Actually, I made this chair for Mr. Johnson. My family made carriages in Philadelphia, so I have some experience working with wood."

"Very good experience, from the looks of that chair," she responded. "It's beautiful."

"Thank you for the compliment. I hope Mr. Johnson is equally impressed."

"I'm sure he will be," said Grace as she started to move away, then stopped.

"We had a Madison Carriage when we lived in Richmond. One of yours, I presume."

"Most assuredly," responded Frank, searching his memory. *Did I deliver a carriage to the Saulsbys? I would definitely remember having seen her before.*

Frank smiled at Grace. He was glad for the praise and an opportunity to talk to her. It pleased him that the Saulsbys had owned one of his carriages, even though he didn't remember delivering one to them personally. *I'm glad she didn't inquire why I made the chair. I wouldn't want to lie to her.* (The chair contained a hidden metal compartment under the seat.)

*****

When Frank first approached Mr. Johnson about his desire to more fully secure the mine's payroll and silver, he discovered Mr. Johnson was aware that large banks had more than one place to store money, but the bank in Wylerton was only a small branch and therefore only had the one vault. The chair was one of the solutions. Hank made the metal compartment, and let Frank work in the back of his shop to do all the woodwork and upholstery. Only paper money was to be stored in the metal compartment, so even if it were tipped over, the contents would not be detected and the metal would protect it being destroyed even in a fire. Hank was working on another metal vault to be concealed in a wall panel in Mr. Johnson's office. Frank planned to store the silver in it while he was building a special wagon to ship it to Denver. So far, his riders had been making the journey safely. This had been accomplished by carefully randomizing the trips and only carrying small amounts of money and silver. The Clarke Lumber Mill was sending wagons full of lumber to Denver on a regular basis. Eventually, Frank planned to ship larger loads in the special wagons he was making for the Clarkes. Outlaws had stopped one of the Clarke's wagons, but when they found it only contained lumber, they left the drivers unharmed. Frank hoped his luck would hold when he started adding the silver to the lumber shipments. By housing the silver and money in his secret compartments, he hoped they would go undetected. He knew there was good communication between outlaw gangs, and since they were not interested in lumber, ideally, the wagons would be left alone. Only Mr. Clarke and his son knew the wagons were being built. Even with this part of the West getting more settled and his hope the outlaw gangs were becoming less of a threat, he wanted to take every precaution to make sure the silver arrived in Denver safely. The route between Denver and Wylerton was getting well-traveled which was both an advantage and a disadvantage. Outlaws took a bigger risk of being caught on a well-traveled road, but it was also easy pickings for lazy gangs who were willing to take the chance with a quick snatch and grab. Frank was counting on them not stopping a wagon load of lumber to see if it was carrying anything else because if the hidden silver was discovered all his work would be for naught and the Clarke's drivers would be at greater risk. He was grateful Mr. Clarke was willing to participate in this cooperative enterprise. But then again, since the mine would pay them well, the financial benefit was worth the risk.

*****

A few days later, on her way home from the schoolhouse, Grace saw the corral at the livery stables was full of new horses. She walked over to it and stood on the bottom rung of the fence to get a better look. There were several excellent-looking animals in the bunch. They reminded her of their horses in Richmond. *I loved our horses. I still miss Bessey.* She remembered crying herself to sleep the day she had to sell Bessey. Her father, not knowing what their circumstances would be, assured her she would be able to get another horse once they got settled. But their house was too close to town to really need a horse and there were no riding parks in Wylerton, so she hadn't insisted on it. Besides, she wasn't sure any other horse could replace Bessey. However, seeing these horses made her want to ride again.

"Joe Nelson has gotten some good-looking horses don't you think?"

This time, Grace didn't need to look at the man who had come up next to her. She could tell by the sound of his voice and the feel of those silk threads reaching out to attach him to her that it was Frank Madison.

"He has," she answered, without turning to look at him.

"I've lost two really fine horses since leaving Philadelphia. I haven't replaced the last one yet. (Grace detected a sadness in his voice.) The first one died falling off a mountain trail and the other broke his leg a few of months ago and I had to put him down. I was very glad to see this bunch show up in Nelson's stables. Have you knowledge of horses, Miss Saulsby?"

"Yes, we had some excellent horses in Richmond. I love horses, but I had to sell my beloved Bessey when we moved out here," said Grace. Frank notice a slight edge in her voice.

She loves horses, thought Frank with a smile.

"If you were going to buy one of those horses," he asked, "Which one would it be?"

"The chestnut with the dark mane and tail."

"You have a good eye, Miss Saulsby. That's the very horse I just purchased. I've named him Pilot. What was it about him that attracted your notice?"

"He has healthy-looking hair and good muscle tone. He seems to be alert and aware of his surroundings and he carries himself well."

"That's an impressive observation," responded Frank. "How did you come by your knowledge of horses?"

"I've read several books," responded Grace.

"I see." said Frank. *A beautiful woman with a propensity for learning. I like that.*

Grace turned to look at him. It was a mistake. His penetrating look always threw her off balance. She quickly turned her attention back to the horses.

"Judging from your accurate observations, those must have been well written books," he continued. "When I was growing up, I spent a lot of time at a livery stable and thought I learned a lot about horses. Then on my way out here, I spent several months at a horse ranch. The owner had more knowledge of horses than I knew existed." Frank then proceeded to share some of the things Bill Hartman had taught him about how to judge a horse's personality and what to look for to determine if the horse would become a friend and partner or just a means of transportation, etc. As he talked, the sound of his voice spread warmth through Grace's very soul and his nearness caused a sense of home to wash over her, almost overpowering the fascinating information he was sharing. It took her a minute to realize he had asked her a question.

"Pardon me?" she said.

"I asked if there were any of these other horses you like."

After a minute's contemplation, she answered, "The bay with the white sock."

"Yes, that, too, is a very fine animal. What is it you like about that horse?"

Grace had been watching it for several minutes.

"She's not only aware of her surroundings but she seems to be mindful of the other horses. Almost like she is mothering them."

"Since you are a good judge of horses and owned horses in Richmond, why don't you own one now?"

"We live too close to town and there's no place around here to ride," was her answer.

"Miss Saulsby, you must be joking. Why, you can ride a hundred miles in almost any direction without running into a fence."

"Yes, but I wouldn't feel safe riding in the open unsettled country. In Richmond we had riding trails and parks."

"Yes, of course. Perhaps when I get Pilot trained I could show you and your brother the beauty of this unsettled country."

"Perhaps," she answered, surprised that idea was extremely welcoming and by how much she hoped he would remember his offer. She started thinking about riding again and about making herself a split skirt. *Mrs. Davies and the other women I've seen riding sit astride. I haven't seen any of them using a sidesaddle.* Interestingly, as she contemplated such an outing, the thought of riding in the open countryside with Frank Madison didn't seem at all like a frightening prospect. They stood together for several more minutes watching the horses. As Grace thought about the things Frank told her about what qualities made a horse a good partner, she remembered the affection that existed between her and Bessey and realized it was because of Bessey's gentle and sweet personality that they had been so attached to each other. The memory brought tears to her eyes.

"Is there something wrong?" asked Frank.

"No, I'm all right. You just made me think of the horse I had back home. I've just now realized why I loved her so much. Thank you for the information you've shared." Suddenly, Grace realized she was feeling comfortable in Frank's presence and it startled her.

"You'll have to excuse me, Mr. Madison. I must be going," she said.

"Good day to you, then," he said with a tender smile.

She turned away quickly before he could see that she was completely undone by a smile that made his eyes dance like water on a hot skillet and in fact by his very presence. Contemplation about Frank's varying effects on her made her wonder why his suggestion to take Charlie and her riding was a welcome idea. *Why does riding in the open country with Mr. Madison seem so appealing? I wish I understood my feelings toward him.*

On the way home, she stopped in the mercantile.

"Hi, Mrs. Perkins," said Grace as she walked up to the counter, smiling. "I would like to purchase a pair of riding boots."

Mrs. Perkins, puzzled by her cheerfulness, measured her feet, but after checking her supplies couldn't find Grace's size.

"I'll have to order some for you," she said. "It will be about two weeks. Are you planning to get a horse?"

"Not yet, but I thought I'd get used to the boots. The riding boots I brought from Virginia aren't like these. Women there ride sidesaddles and didn't need the kind of boots they wear here."

"Yes," said Mrs. Perkins. "I gave up riding since coming here. Mr. Perkins and I were too busy running the store when we first got here, and then I got too old to learn a different way of sitting on a horse."

Grace picked out the style of boot she wanted and bought three large potatoes.

"Thank you very much, Mrs. Perkins," she said happily as she left.

Having never seen Grace in such a cheerful mood and noticing the bounce in her step as she walked out of the store, Beth Ann thought, *I've never seen her so happy. I wonder if she's in love.*

As she was walking home, Grace took a deep breath and raised her eyes to the mountains. *Okay, they are quite beautiful.* When she got home, she rushed upstairs and dug out her dark blue linen riding habit. *The top is too warm for summer but there is enough material on the bottom to turn it into a split skirt and I have plenty of blouses.* She was pleased she decided to bring the habit. It would be a lot easier to make alterations than start from scratch.

After Grace left, Frank remained at the corral for several more minutes. He finally spotted what he was looking for. The dapple gray was a bit beat up. She had several scars on her neck and a chunk missing from one ear, but the animal was otherwise strong, healthy, and very alert. Frank watched her interact with the other horses and noticed that she, like the horse with the white sock, was gracious about moving when her space was infringed upon by other horses that were heedless of those around them. It made him wonder how she came by her scars.

He went into the livery to talk to Joe Nelson.

"Hey, Joe. I also want the bay with the white sock and the dapple gray with the chewed up ear."

"Yeah, that dapple gray is pretty tore up. I'll give her to you for two dollars, but that bay is going to cost you."

"It doesn't matter," answered Frank. "I'll take them both in addition to the one I already purchased. And will you outfit them with saddles and everything? Also, I'll need you to house them for a while until I get my corral finished and my barn raised."

"Okay," answered Joe. "That won't be a problem. I'll get right on it."

*****

The next afternoon as Grace was on her way home from the school, Minnie Stewart called after her. "Hi, Grace," she greeted. "A few of us are getting together next week, at Claire's house to make a quilt to auction off at the Midsummer Festival. Would you like to join us?"

"Of course," answered Grace. "I've heard about the festival. It's been a few years since I've done any quilting, but I'm sure I still remember how. Thank you for inviting me. What time should I be there?"

"We want to start at ten. With five of us working on it, we are hoping to get it done before dark. Claire and her mother are going to have it all set up for us."

"Okay, I'll leave school a little early. I have my own needles, but should I also bring thread and scissors?"

"That would be good if you could. Just white thread should be fine. See you there then. Bye." She was off before Grace could question her about the Midsummer Festival, but as she thought about Minnie's invitation on the way home, she decided she should be more friendly. She was becoming more aware that her life in Richmond was in her past and that she should be taking more of an interest in her future in Wylerton. The thought was not exactly a joyful one but she decided it would be a lot better to make the most of it instead of ignoring reality.

17

Frank's Barn Raising

Early on the first Saturday of June the whole town showed up for Frank's barn raising. Mrs. Perkins, Betty Packer, and Joe Nelson's wife Lucy had organized a picnic. Grace agreed to bring four loaves of bread. Everyone was grateful that the weather was perfect. Since Grace had never been to such an event, she was surprised and delighted by the friendly atmosphere and the excitement in the air. It seemed an impossible task to build a barn in one day, so she was anxious to watch how it was done. She wouldn't have been surprised to see the men Frank worked with in the mine or his friends Hank, Willie, and Joe there, but she was sure every man in town, including some of the miners from the Tucker Mine, had come to help. It said a lot about Frank's popularity. It hadn't gotten past Grace that he was generally well liked and respected, but this was beyond what she had ever imagined. It was a unique awakening and gave her pause as she reflected on what she knew about him personally. She had to admit to herself that even the time he carried her across the street, his behavior had always been that of a gentleman.

By noon when everyone took a break to eat, the frames for four walls were lying on the ground around the foundation that Frank and Willie Barton had previously built. It was fascinating how the men paired up in teams, and Grace was impressed that they all seemed to know exactly what to do as each team put one of the four walls together. After the break, the children were taken aside by some of the moms to play games with Claire and Mr. Jenkins. While the men lay on the ground for a while resting, Grace helped Mrs. Perkins and some of the other women clean up. Dishes were washed in big tubs on the back of a wagon and set out to dry on another. Grace was enchanted by the organization of the affair but didn't realize until Hank called that it was time for the raising how much more fascinated she would be.

The teams that were organized for each side took their positions. There were about fifteen men for each team. Mr. Johnson was asked to sound the start. Minnie Steward and Priscilla Jones were cheering for the Clarke brothers who were on one of the teams and the men on each of the other teams had wives and family members cheering them on. Grace was glad the Perkins were cheering for Frank's team which consisted of Charlie and her father, Hank, Willie, Joe Nelson, and some other men she didn't know. As she and Beth Ann Perkins stood together watching, it made her realize how much she had grown to like Beth Ann and the other townspeople she was getting to know. Then Grace watched as each team participated in the most exciting feat she had ever beheld. She was drawn into the excitement of the event, cheering along with the other women as each of the four sides of the barn was raised up and hammered into place.

"We won!" cried Charlie, as Frank and Willie put the last nails of their wall in place. It had been close, but Mr. Johnson declared Frank's team the winners by less than thirty seconds. Grace didn't even think about the hugs going around until she hugged Frank. It felt totally different from the hugs she had given her father and Charlie and the other men on their team. Again, physical contact with Frank Madison made her skin tingle and sent a thrill through her that excited her every nerve. She didn't know how long she was in his arms. Everything fell away—time, space, the world around her. She was aware only of him and a feeling of belonging. When he released her, she felt that same sense of abandonment she had experienced before. She looked into his eyes and was sure he was trying to tell her something, but someone called his name and Lucy was saying something about getting the rafters up before they lost the light. The moment was over quickly and Grace was left to ponder the experience as the men went to work on the rafters.

With the women bringing food and Claire and Mr. Jenkins organizing games for the children, it had been a wonderful community event, and by dusk, Frank had the framework for a new barn. With the work done, they all sat around in small groups talking. Some of the men started playing banjos and harmonicas, and some of the women started singing folk songs. As she participated in these activities, Grace became aware that she was beginning to focus more on the people she was getting to know and like and less on the drab appearance of the town.

*****

With his barn finished and his corral built, Frank decided it was time to bring home his horses. He and Pilot were getting along well. He was enjoying training him. Although no horse would replace the love he had for Target, Frank was forming a good bond with Pilot and noticed the horse had a unique sensitivity to his moods. He was sure that over time they would form the kind of bond necessary for them to become partners. Also, after personally training Tabby and Gray, he was satisfied with the purchase of each of these horses as well. *Grace did a good job picking out Tabby. She will be a perfect companion for her.*

Working with the horses had been something Frank looked forward to each evening and it brought a joy to his heart he hadn't experienced in a long time. When he went to the livery to settle his account, he wasn't really surprised at the amount of money he had to fork out, and although it put a dent in his savings, it was going to be worth it. Now he could go riding with Grace and Charlie, and he still had plenty of money to build a house. *Besides,* he thought, *Pilot, Tabby, and Gray are a good start to seeing the dream come true that I've had for a long time.* The horses were the start of his herd, and the gear part of an investment in what he hoped would be his future with Grace.

After several weeks of exploring his land, Frank figured out he would be able to sustain a good size herd. He decided the high meadow would be great for summer grazing. It had only one easy access and that passage was visible from where he was building the house. He also had enough lower pastures to graze the horses the rest of the year. Happy with these aspects of his future, Grace was the only uncertainty. He wanted more than anything for his relationship with her to grow, but since that wasn't a sure thing yet, it caused him a good deal of anxiety.

18

A Close Encounter

Saturday morning Grace rushed through her housework. With the laundry done the day before, she had a good start on the day. Charlie, who didn't have to study on Saturday, had already taken off for the Davies Ranch, and her dad was going to spend the morning in the office. She had mentioned to him more than once he really needed to hire a secretary. By ten thirty, Grace was ready to head for the meadow on the other side of the woods across the river. She took a basket for the wild strawberries she was going to pick, a slice of bread, and an apple in case she wanted to linger after picking the berries. It was a bit late in the season but she was hopeful that she could still find some in the little meadow. She still needed to make jam. She had to admit it was a pleasant walk to the river. The McNeals who had lived here before must have gone to the river on a regular basis. The path was well worn and easy to follow and the rope bridge made for an easy river crossing.

As she drew near the river, she looked across the large field that stretched far to the south. She could see the place where Frank was building a house. The foundation must have been finished because two of the outside walls were framed up. There were several men there working with him. Although they were quite far away, she recognized Willie Barton, one of the mine workers, and Hank Wilder, the blacksmith. Grace was pleased to see this was going to be more than one of those shabby little three-room houses like the ones in town. She again reflected at how fortunate they were that their house had been part of the purchase of the title company. Having come from Chicago, the McNeals knew what a decent house was supposed to be like. It looked as if Frank Madison did also.

Grace stood watching the men work for a while. They seemed to be enjoying themselves. She could hear their laughter and the cheerfulness of their conversation. She was continually being made aware that Mr. Madison was a well-liked person. It was a warm day and none of them had shirts on. She would have been embarrassed if she had been any closer. She was close enough, however, to see that all of the men had beautifully muscular bodies. She wasn't surprised at seeing Hank Wilder without a shirt. Being a blacksmith, he hardly ever wore a shirt, but seeing Mr. Madison shirtless, well, that was certainly a treat. *It's exciting to watch him working.* Grace brought herself up and shook herself mentally at that thought, then gave herself a scold for staring. She made her way to the river, crossed the rope bridge, and walked into the woods. The sun filtering through the trees and the warmth of the day allowed Grace to relax. Here she could let go of some of the depression that still lingered in her heart. *I will probably never see Richmond again or live in a place of culture and beauty,* she thought. *I need to start focusing on the positive things about Wylerton.* Frank Madison came to mind. *Other than Mr. Madison.*

Surprisingly, she found more strawberries than she had expected. After filling her basket, she sat in a sunny spot in the meadow to eat her apple and bread, but the quiet and the warmth of the day made her drowsy.

Before she realized it, the sunny spot was gone and the air was quite a bit cooler. Grace could see from the developing clouds there was every indication a storm was approaching. She started hurrying back to the river. *How long was I sleeping? How could the weather change so much? It was such a pleasant sunny day. You can never be sure a day here will end the way it starts.* The rain began to fall just as she crossed the rope bridge. It was coming down in buckets and she was instantly drenched. Her straw bonnet flopped down in front of her face and tripping over her soaking wet skirt, she fell to her knees. She was trying to stand when she felt herself being grabbed by the waist.

"Miss Saulsby, let me give you a ride home."

It was Frank Madison. How had he known she was there?

Grace knew it would be foolish to refuse his help. The day having been so warm, she hadn't bothered with a shawl. She was already soaked to the skin and shivering, she removed the drenched bonnet. But when she looked at the horse, it had no saddle.

"Oh, I can't ride a horse without a saddle."

"Don't worry, I'll hold you."

Frank threw himself onto Pilot, then reached down and pulled Grace up in front of him. She clutched the basket to her chest and quickly covered it with her bonnet. Frank put one arm around her waist and pulled her snug against his chest, guiding the horse with his other hand. At first, Grace was shocked. He was not wearing a shirt and her wet clothes were plastered to her skin. *We might as well be riding together naked.* However, the first order of business was to stay on the horse which Frank immediately nudged into a full gallop.

The noise of the downpour and the embarrassment of the situation discouraged Grace from attempting conversation and it didn't take long for them to reach her house. Frank urged his horse up next to the porch and promptly deposited Grace on it. Then without a word or a second glance, he took off. Grace rushed into the house, glad to be home and alone. She ran into the kitchen, set the basket and her bonnet on the table, then hurried to her room, only to have the mirror confirm what she already knew. Her wet cotton blouse and underclothes were virtually transparent. She was mortified. *How am I ever to face him again?* She quickly shed the wet clothes and put on her warmest robe. First, she took her sopping wet clothes into the laundry room, then went to the kitchen to inspect the strawberries. She was grateful to find she hadn't lost too many when she fell, but the jam would have to wait. She felt tired and chilled. The day had been too warm to have a fire burning, so she grabbed a quilt and snuggled up on the couch.

Her first thought was that she would never recover from the experience. *How had he even been there?* As she replayed the day's events in her mind, however, she began to realize that if she could see the men working on Frank's house, most likely they had also spotted her. She also reflected on how quickly he had lifted her up onto the horse and how quickly he had taken off after setting her down on the porch. He *knew* it was an embarrassing situation. He did everything he could make it less so. She realized now that he hadn't looked at her after setting her down on the porch. Then she remembered the day he had carried her across the street. *Mr. Frank Madison might be a scruffy-looking man but he is without question a gentleman.* Grace wasn't sure how she felt about this realization. However, she decided she was going to get to know him better.

19

Realizations

It was getting harder and harder to get Grace Saulsby out of his mind. He had been thrilled to see her watching him working on his house. *Did that mean she was interested or at least curious? Did she feel what I felt when she hugged me at the barn raising? How can I further my relationship with her?* These were all questions he couldn't answer, but he was glad he had seen her. He was right about her not being prepared for the storm. He wished he'd had time to grab a shirt, but those clouds opened up so fast he was lucky to have gotten to her when he did. *She would have been chilled to the bone if she had had to walk home in that downpour. She felt mighty good in my arms. So soft. So feminine. I hope she's going to be all right and not become ill. Is she going to be too shy to ever look me in the face again when she discovered how transparent her wet blouse was? It was all I could do not to give into the desire to linger on her feminine beauty. Grace Saulsby is definitely setting up house in my heart.* Then he thought, *I'm glad I didn't have time to grab a shirt. The feel of her against my skin was delicious. If only I could always hold her like that.*

It was still raining when he got back to his house after dropping Grace off. Hank and Willie and the others had gone home knowing the rain had put an end to their work. He didn't feel like going back to his room in the hotel. The barn would be just fine. *Luxurious compared to sleeping on the plains in Kansas during the winter.* As he was settling down for the night, Charlie and the Davies boy came to mind. He decided to see if they would like to hire out to help him. Perhaps Charlie was the way to Grace's heart.

*****

Frank would have been delighted to know Grace's attitude and feelings for him were gradually taking a turn for the better. She realized it herself when she and Minnie Stewart, Priscilla Jones, Mrs. Johnson, and Claire got together a few days after her embarrassing experience to make the quilt for the Midsummer Festival auction. All Priscilla and Minnie could talk about was how handsome and wonderful the Clarke brothers were.

"I think Roger is the dreamiest man that ever lived," sighed Minnie. "I'll just die if he doesn't ask me to dance."

Grace didn't have any doubt that he would. With her curly blonde hair, she looked like a porcelain doll. Grace thought she had the brains of a porcelain doll but then quickly let go of that unchristian thought.

"You can have Roger," replied Priscilla. "I'll take Jeff any day. He is so strong and handsome. Even though Roger is older, Jeff is taller and stronger."

"How do you know he's stronger?" cried Minnie. "Working in the lumber mill is just as hard as working in a mine. I'll bet he is just as strong."

"Maybe you will get to dance with both of them," said Claire.

There was a time when Grace had wondered why Claire, like Minnie and Priscilla, didn't swoon over the Clarke brothers until several weeks ago when she became aware of Claire's interest in the schoolteacher, Mr. Jenkins.

When Grace told her about helping Mr. Jenkins tutor the young students, Claire was enthralled.

"Oh, I think that would be a wonderful thing to do. How did you come to be doing that?" she inquired.

"I just offered my services, and he was delighted for the help. You should go talk to him. If my father doesn't hire a secretary I may have to start working for him and give up helping at the school."

It wasn't more than two days later that Claire came to the school. Mr. Jenkins was more than happy to have her help. A few days after Claire started working there, it wasn't too hard to see that there was a mutual attraction between them. Mr. Jenkins was of average height and on the slender side, but with his dark hair, light blue eyes, and even features, he was quite handsome. Grace hoped the relationship would bloom. *Claire is a pretty, delicate girl and much too smart for either of the Clarke brothers.*

She was brought back to the present by Minnie's remark that being the oldest Roger would be the one to inherit the mill and Jeff would always have to work in the mine.

"You don't know that," said Priscilla. "When the mill expands, maybe they will need Jeff to come back to work there or maybe he is saving his money and will buy his own business. There are a lot of people moving to California, you know. Maybe we will get married and move to California." As Grace listened to the two girls banter back and forth about the Clarke brothers—who was the better-looking, strongest, smartest, etc.—she was glad the quilt was almost done.

It occurred to her during this conversation that she was no longer concerned about Frank's looks. Oh, sure, his appearance had put her off at first, but now she realize his looks didn't matter to her. Well, that was mostly true. She liked the sparkle of his eyes when he smiled and he had an attractive nose. She liked that he was strong and well-built and how she felt in his arms. After seeing him again in church, she was starting to get over the humiliation of the rainy day experience, especially as she realized she liked being held by him. Also, when she thought back on that day when he was working with Willie and Hank and the others, she remembered these men hadn't just been working together, they had been enjoying each other's company. She was made aware at his barn raising, Frank was well-liked by not only the mine workers but also the townspeople. Everyone spoke well of him. She was reminded of the scripture in the Bible about not judging a person by their outward appearance. She guessed she was learning that lesson when it came to Frank Madison. There was something more to him than met the eye. He was more than a mine worker. Even more than the manager. *He is very intelligent and very much a gentleman. Even if he isn't that handsome, he does have very expressive eyes.* On the way home from the quilting party, she was suddenly aware that she was looking forward to the journey of getting to know him better, but she also realized she forgot to ask about the Midsummer Festival. *I guess they all just assumed I knew about it.*

20

A Conversation

Allen Saulsby was still concerned about his daughter. Although lately they were not as frequent, her melancholy moods still worried him. He wondered if it had been a mistake taking her away from the only environment she had known. He fretted about the responsibilities that had been dumped on her after his wife's death, especially when it came to raising her brother. However, when he discovered she and Charlie liked eating finger food while they were engaged in their studies, he started eating his midday meal more often at Betty Packer's Cafe. The food was good and he was happy to relieve Grace of the chore of preparing the meal. It pleased Allen that his son had finally given into being taught by his sister. He knew Grace had an insatiable desire for learning and the present arrangement seemed to be proving beneficial to both his children.

Frank Madison was sitting alone when Allen walked into the cafe.

"May I join you?" he asked.

"Please do," responded Frank.

Betty came to the table promptly after Allen sat down.

"What can I get you today, Mr. Saulsby?"

"The roast beef special will be fine. Thank you, Betty." Then turning his attention to Frank, he said, "Several years ago, Madison carriages were becoming quite popular in Richmond. In fact, we owned one. Is there any connection?"

"Yes," responded Frank. "My grandfather started working for the Buckner Carriage Company when he was a boy. Mr. Buckner didn't have any children, so my grandfather took over when the old man passed away. When my dad got old enough to partner with my grandfather, they changed the name. My dad was a talented artisan and made several improvements in the carriage design. I think those things and the integrity of his craftsmanship made us very successful. I started working with them when I was ten or eleven. As I got older, my father discovered I was good with people. He sent me out to expand our territory. Richmond became one of our new areas. That's when we discovered the fine quality of the hardware produced by the Richmond Brass Works. We started getting all of our hardware from them. As it was easier for me to make the long journey to Richmond, it became my responsibility to deliver the carriages and buy the brass fittings. I traveled there two or three times a year. Your daughter told me you owned one of our carriages. I don't remember delivering it to you."

"That's because I acquired it as a result of a loan default," explained Allen. "I understand you lost your family. What happened?" asked Allen.

Frank explained about the train accident.

"Richmond is a beautiful city," commented Frank. "How is your family adjusting to living here in Wylerton?"

"My son Charles loves it here. But my daughter Grace is struggling."

"This country is very different, but it has its own unique beauty. One day maybe she will come to appreciate it," commented Frank, then realized the remark reflected a deep-rooted concern of his own about Grace.

"I hope so," responded Allen.

"It didn't take me long after my family died to discover there was no joy in carrying on the family business alone," continued Frank. "And, much like you, I needed a change. I've always had a love of horses, and this country is a perfect area for a horse ranch. The challenges of striking out on my own have been good for me. New experiences have taught me much about myself. One of the most important things I've learned is that family is important to me." *Your daughter is important to me.* "I think there are advantages to raising a family here." *Raising a family with your daughter would be a dream come true,* he thought.

Out loud, he said, "Perhaps your daughter will come to enjoy the new experiences she is having. A while ago I made her an offer to take your son and her out to explore the country. If she agrees to the outings, would that meet with your approval? Maybe that will help her come to appreciate what this area has to offer."

I hope he is right, thought Allen. Out loud, he said, "I'm sure Charlie would be more than happy to spend his time that way. I'd be surprised if Grace accepts your offer, but if she does, you have my approval. You seem to be doing an excellent job managing the mine. How did you come by doing that?"

"I have a degree in accounting. When I arrived in Wylerton, Mr. Jackson and his brother were looking for an accountant. I wanted a job, so I offered my services. When their company in Denver started demanding more of their attention, one of the brothers was going to stay and run the mine, but for some reason, they asked me to be the foreman and handed over the management to me so they could both return to Denver. I guess they figured my accounting experience made up for my other deficiencies. It's turned out to be beneficial for both of us."

"I see," answered Allen, wondering what deficiencies Frank saw in himself. Everything he knew about the young man showed him to be both capable and honorable.

"You must have a talent for organization and working with people," responded Allen. "The mine seems to be doing very well."

"It is. Hiring part-time men has proved very effective. I've paired the new men up with the experienced miners, and that is working well. However, I think the fact that the mine has rich veins of silver is the main reason. The Jacksons can pay the miners well because profits are good."

"I see you started building your house," Allen said.

"I have, but it's slow going. I only have evenings and Saturdays free, you know. I'm thinking about hiring extra help. Do you think your son would be interested?"

"Very much. Ever since Charlie was young we had to come up with various activities to keep him both mentally and physically busy."

Allen knew that in addition to his barn, Frank was building a good size house and stables on the ten thousand acres he had purchased (and paid for in cash). He was impressed that a young man with obvious means would take on the responsibilities of being a mine foreman. He was impressed with his drive to establish a home and put down roots. As their conversation drifted into other areas, Allen was further impressed with Frank's scope of knowledge and easy manner. He liked him and was sure Frank would be a good influence on Charlie. Neither man was fully aware of how entwined each of their interests were in Grace.

21

Things Coming Together

Once Claire started working at the school, Grace realized she was not really needed anymore and therefore told Mr. Jenkins she was going to let Claire take over so she could start helping her father at his office. He still hadn't hired a secretary, and every time she stopped by, the disorder drove her crazy. She hadn't informed her father of her plans to become his secretary, but she knew once she started working there and he saw how helpful she could be, he would relent. That Friday on her way home from the school, she was reflecting on how much she enjoyed teaching but then started thinking about all the things she planned to do for her father on Monday and realized she was looking forward to that experience, also.

"Miss Saulsby."

Grace froze. She took a deep breath. She didn't need to turn around to know who had addressed her. The sound of his voice was like music. She was suddenly aware of two conflicting instincts—one to flee, the other to throw herself into his arms. She was confused by this reaction to his presence.

"I haven't seen your brother in a while. He is no longer attending school, is he?" Frank knew her brother wasn't attending school but thought it best not to be too familiar. However, since Wylerton wasn't a very big town, Grace wasn't surprised at Frank noticing Charlie wasn't attending school anymore.

"No," she responded. "He is studying at home now."

"I see. My guess is that he was the oldest boy in the school and, if I'm not mistaken, a bit taller than Mr. Jenkins." He paused. When she didn't respond, he went on. "The reason I enquire is because I could use some help building my house. It would only be in the evenings and perhaps Saturdays. Did your brother want to work in the mine because he needs the money or because he just wanted to get out of going to school?"

"He was just trying to get out of going to school."

Grace said all this without turning to look at Frank. She knew he might think her rude, but she was afraid if she looked at him he would perceive how much he affected her.

"How do you feel about your brother working? I understand you have taken on the responsibility of being a mother to him. Do you object to him working or did you just not want him to work in the mine?"

"I just didn't want him working in the mine. Charles would probably be delighted to have a job. He likes keeping active. You should talk to him and, of course, my father."

"Thank you. I have talked to your father but I wanted to make sure it would meet with your approval, also."

Grace turned to look at him as she started to depart and regretted it. The look in his dark blue eyes was intense and drew her in like a magnet. She couldn't look away. She didn't know how long it took to break the spell.

"I think Charlie would most likely jump at the chance to help build your house," she answered, then hurried away. Every time they were together, she felt a little more need to belong to him. It was almost as if they were destined to be together. Since she didn't understand these feelings, they frightened her.

*****

Frank realized his need for Grace to be part of his life grew every time their eyes made contact. She seemed to belong to him; it's been that way from the start. His instincts told him she was also feeling the draw but had a feeling she was resisting it. Frank stood there watching her; she had such natural grace. He was mesmerized by her pull on him even as the distance between them grew. Since he had a feeling his presence disturbed her, he waited to see if she would stamp her foot as she had the time he had carried her across the street. She didn't. He smiled.

*****

Allen Saulsby was a man of few words. However, he was observant. When Charlie first started going to work at four in the afternoon, he would come home too tired to do anything but throw himself in bed and sleep until around eleven o'clock. He would then wake up and eat the meal Grace had placed on the table by his bed and go back to sleep until eight the next morning at which time he would dive into his schoolwork. But in spite of this exhausting schedule, he seemed enthusiastic about it and he was eager to go to work each night. Because he wasn't shirking his studies, Grace didn't complain. After a couple of weeks, Charlie got used to the work and was again able to join them for dinner. Allen also noticed his son was even more interested in his studies. He knew Frank was a well-educated man and was thankful that he was having such a good influence on his son.

It also didn't get past Allen that there was no longer a spider problem in the kitchen and that Grace hung on every word about how "Last night Frank showed me how to do this" and "Frank told me about that" and "Frank said this" and "Frank knows all about…" This observation made him smile to himself. He hoped that Grace's obvious interest in Frank Madison would ease her discontent about her life in Wylerton. He had questioned more than once his choice about the move. Unlike his son who had taken to a Western lifestyle without a hitch and seemed to be growing and thriving, Grace was still struggling with this new way of life and Allen was concerned for her future. At twenty-two, she would have been in the very thick of Richmond's social life and perhaps already married. He had never told Grace that one of the deciding factors to leave Richmond was his strong dislike for the Sullivan family and his concern when their son Stuart started taking a particular interest in her. The young man himself was handsome and very charming, but Allen did not want his daughter attached to the family. Grace was a smart well-educated woman but he knew she was unaware of how the Sullivans treated their former slaves and he was afraid of her getting emotionally involved with their son. But what of her future here? He was glad when she started helping at the school. But other than that, she spent most of her time at home keeping house, studying with Charlie, or reading. It wasn't a typical way for a girl her age to spend her time, and he would like to have seen her engaging more with people her own age. He wondered if maybe Frank Madison was the cure to the melancholy she often demonstrated. He had not missed that there was something going on between them. He wasn't exactly sure what it was, but he was hopeful it was a good thing.

He enjoyed his conversations with Frank in the cafe. The young man had integrity, a quick mind, and an enthusiasm for life. In fact, Allen Saulsby was pleased by both his children's interest in Mr. Madison. He was impressed with the young man's boldness when he learned Frank was from Philadelphia, and that after his family was killed, he sold their carriage company and his home and worked his way across the country. Allen recognized the journey had turned an already fine man into someone with a wide variety of skills and a rare depth of character. Since Frank worked even when he didn't need to, Allen knew that kind of work ethic would bode well no matter what circumstances he faced. Allen was glad a man of Frank's caliber had also ended up in Wylerton and that Grace seemed to be warming up to the idea of getting to know him. He secretly thought Frank a very good match for Grace. *Maybe coming here was the right thing to do after all. I hope Frank follows through with his plans to show her around the country.*

*****

Her father was surprised when Grace showed up that first day, planning to help in the office for a few hours. But then he remembered that on more than one occasion she told him he needed a

116

secretary. He smiled to himself that she was taking the matter into her own hands.

At first, Grace didn't feel as if she was making much progress. There were piles of filing which needed to be done. There were contracts in various stages of completion that needed to be organized and there was no order to the correspondence that needed to be addressed. For a while, she wondered how her father had managed without her and if she was ever going to make any real difference by just working a couple of hours a day, but gradually things started coming together and she began to feel the work she was doing was important. It wasn't much over a week for Mr. Saulsby to realize how right Grace had been about him needing a secretary. He was amazed that in the short time she had been helping him how well organized his office had become. Before long, the filing was all up to date, he never had to search for the accounts that needed his attention, the letters he needed to address were well organized, and he knew right where to find the contracts for the customers who were scheduled to come into the office that day. Yes, his Grace was quite a smart and talented young woman. He hoped the work she was doing was as much a blessing to her as it was to him.

Once she could see she was making a difference for her father, Grace was glad about her new circumstances. She loved teaching Charlie and often wondered if she would have been able to do it if she and Caroline hadn't studied together the way they did. The evenings before she planned to go to work, she would organize her brother's assignments so she could get him started on his studies in the morning before she left, knowing she didn't have to worry about him staying engaged. Ever since he started working for Frank Madison, Charlie had become an even more eager student. There was no longer a need to prod him to study. After working at the title company for a couple of hours, Grace would come home to discuss his studies before he went to help Frank. She loved that their conversations were becoming deeper and more engaging. And even after spending almost a whole day studying, he was anxious to go work on Frank's house afterward. Grace soon realized Frank was Charlie's hero. She thought about the influence Mr. Madison was having on her brother and wondered what it was that made Charlie so taken with him. From their dinner conversations, she learned that Frank evidently knew a lot about *everything* and could do *everything*. Because of this, she decided she needed to reevaluate her impression of Mr. Madison. *Okay, so I guess I was wrong to have thought he was only a scruffy old miner. Not that I ever thought he was old.*

22

Figuring Things Out

Grace decided it was time to get to know Mr. Madison on a more personal level and not just be learning about him from other people and her brother. *I've got to figure out why he has such a profound effect on me.* A few days later, as she was getting ready to leave her father's office, she saw Frank go into the mercantile. She grabbed her purse and hurried across the street. When she walked in she saw he was chatting with Bob Blackburn, the owner of a dairy farm. She hesitated, not wanting to interrupt their conversation. Then when Frank stepped up to the counter, she eased toward him.

"Hi, Mrs. Perkins," he said. "Do you still have some of those licorice ropes?"

"Why, sure thing, Frank. We wouldn't let our supply run out knowing how much you like them now would we?"

"Then give me a nickel's worth, will ya?" he said, slapping the nickel on the counter.

Grace grabbed a penny out of her purse and purposely dropped it as she approached the counter. Frank heard the coin drop and turned to retrieve it just as Grace was also bending down. Their heads collided, and Grace looked into his eyes and smiled. To her surprise, he quickly put the penny in her hand and left the store without saying a word or even taking his candy. Grace was more than puzzled. She was hurt. *What just happened? I was sure Mr. Madison had an interest in me. Was I wrong? All those times was he just being a gentle-man? Have I done something to offend him?*

She stood there for a minute, shocked. When she came to her senses, she saw that Mrs. Perkins was also surprised by his behavior.

"Well, I declare," said Mrs. Perkins. "What was that all about? Why, I've never seen him behave in such a manner."

"I'm sure I couldn't say," responded Grace.

She really didn't know what to think. As she was recovering from the shock of the whole incident, she noticed his licorice sitting on the counter.

"My brother Charlie works for Mr. Madison," she said. "I could get him to take the licorice to him when he goes to work this afternoon."

"That would be very thoughtful, my dear," replied Mrs. Perkins, as she put the licorice in a bag. "I just don't know what got into him."

"Maybe he just remembered something urgent he needed to do," Grace offered to ease the tension of the situation.

Frank's heart was still pounding, and by the time he reached the blacksmith's shop, he felt out of breath. He'd gotten away as fast as he could, but on the other hand, he was kicking himself for bolting. *What on earth got into me? Well, I know exactly what got into me. My raging desire to take Grace into my arms and kiss her beautiful mouth was what got into me. She's lovely even when she is frowning, but she smiled at me. I wasn't prepared for its effect.* He knew there would have been no way she would forgive him if he had brazenly grabbed her up in his arms and kissed her right there in the mercantile (which is exactly what he craved doing).

"Frank, are you all right?" asked Hank when he saw Frank standing in the doorway breathing like he'd just run a mile.

"I'm fine. I just had a close call with Grace Saulsby. She smiled at me, and I had to get away fast to keep from kissing her in the mercantile. I don't know what's come over me where that girl is concerned."

Hank smiled to himself. He wondered if Frank knew how obvious his attraction to Grace was but decided not to say anything just then.

"Sorry, Hank. I didn't mean to interrupt you."

"You never have to worry about that," said Hank, giving Frank a friendly pat on the back. "I've just about got that vault finished. Do you want to have a look?"

"No, not right now. I'll come back later."

On the way back to the newly constructed mine office with his heart and head still in turmoil, Frank pondered his situation. *I'm going to have to get a grip on myself when it comes to being around that girl or I'll blow any chance I have with her. Maybe I already have, but she should have known better than to smile at me when we were so close. Why did she smile at me? She has always seemed a little hesitant to get to know me. Has something changed and now have I really messed up? The Midsummer Festival is coming up in a week, maybe I can patch things up then. Charlie is only a teenager but he might be able to give me some insight into Grace's feelings. Well, at least her reaction to my uncouth behavior this afternoon.*

Grace was puzzling all the way home. *Have I missed something? He has always been so friendly and shown an interest in getting better acquainted. Has Charlie told Frank something about me that has turned him against me? Perhaps he has gotten discouraged by my standoff-ish disposition toward him and has given up on getting acquainted.* She stamped her foot. *Oh why does life have to be so complicated?*

She was still mulling it through her mind while she was fixing their midday meal and stamped her foot at least twice.

Since it was one of those occasions when her father was home for the afternoon, he asked, "Are we having trouble with spiders again?"

"Yes!" Grace answered emphatically.

Her father chuckled to himself. He suspected her foot stamping might have something to do with Frank Madison. *I'm sure she has some kind of feelings toward him. I wonder what happened between them that has caused the stamping.*

Gratefully, Grace was able to steer the conversation around the things Charlie was learning rather than the work he was doing for Frank. She was still reeling over his behavior earlier that day and didn't want discuss anything that included him. However, by the end of the meal, she had the presence of mind to remember to give Charlie his licorice.

*****

Frank was anxious for Charlie to get to work. It was his hope to discover Grace's reaction to his rude behavior.

When Charlie showed up, Frank was surprised and pleased to be handed the candy he had left on the counter.

"Did you get this from your sister?" he enquired.

"Yeah, she said you forgot to take it when you were in the mercantile."

"Did she say anything else?"

"No, but she was in kind of a huff for some reason. She stamped her foot a lot while she was fixing luncheon."

"She stamped her foot, *huh*? Just what does that mean Charlie?" Frank asked, curious to learn more about Grace and this behavior he'd witnessed.

"Well, whenever she is upset about something she has a habit of stamping her foot."

Frank recalled her doing that the day he carried her across the muddy street and guessed she had been torn between being embarrassed and grateful. It made him smile.

"Did she say why she was upset?"

"No, but I think it was something that happened earlier today because she has been in a really good mood lately."

"Why do you think she has been in a good mood?"

"Oh, I don't know. She really likes that I'm working harder on my studies but that's because I want to be as smart as you, and she likes helping our dad at the office. She really liked working in the school with Mr. Jenkins, but Claire Johnson is doing that now, so Grace is helping our dad. I think she just likes having something to do besides housework. We had a maid in Richmond but Mom made Grace learn to keep house and cook. She was mad at the time because she thought it beneath her station, but our mom taught her those things so, 'she would be a capable and independent woman.' At least that's what she told me when I asked why she had to do housework. She couldn't go to college like she wanted to, of course, but Dad bought her a ton of books so she could study on her own. She and her best friend Caroline used to study as if they were going to college. They even made up tests for each other. I think that's why she is so concerned about my education. She has a hard time understanding why anyone would not want to learn as much as they possibly could. I'm pretty sure she plans on reading every one of our books that she hasn't already studied."

Frank was grateful to learn all of this about Grace. He could sense from their various interactions that she was intelligent and it pleased him to learn how enterprising she had been about wanting to be educated, but it didn't solve the problem of how he was going to mend the fence where she was concerned. He certainly wasn't going to tell Charlie he rushed out of the mercantile to keep himself from kissing his sister, but he wished Charlie could have given him some information about that.

Instead, he said, "Your sister is right, you know. Anyone is foolish who passes up an education."

"How come you are so smart, Frank?" asked Charlie. "I thought people worked in the mine because they couldn't do anything else."

"That's a misconception, Charlie. Willie used to be a cowboy, but mining pays better, so he changed jobs. Lots of the men work in the mine because of the pay. I've done lots of different things during my life. Back in Philadelphia where I grew up, my family owned a carriage shop. That's when I learned how to work with wood and do upholstery. I started learning about horses while I was growing up because I loved horses, so I spent a lot of time at the livery stables near our shop. My dad sent me to college to study accounting and finances. Like your sister, he thought getting an education was very important. My studies helped us manage our business better. I've worked in a bank, and I've learned to use a gun and hunt because I didn't get to Wylerton by taking the train to Denver and coming up here in a stagecoach like you. It took me over three years walking and traveling on horseback to get across the country. Toward the start of my journey, I stayed at a horse ranch for several months and learned to train horses and make saddles. I learned a lot about myself during that time and how to take care of myself in various situations. It's important to take advantage of every opportunity to learn new things. But I've never worked in a mine before. So when I started my job with the Jackson Brothers, I decided to learn about mining. However, I don't just work in the mine, you know, and my job includes more than just taking care of the finances. I'm in charge of the whole operation of the mine. I work in the mine a couple of days a week to get to know the men better and keep track of the conditions in the mine and the equipment. I have to monitor the men's health and make sure everyone is getting along and doing their job. I think of doing new things as getting a practical education and not just learning from books, like you helping me build this house. You study from books, then come here and learn by doing. Both kinds of education are important. Life itself is an education, if you pay attention."

"Wow," replied Charlie. "No wonder you're so smart."

"Only because, like your sister, I enjoy learning and take every advantage to do so."

"Well, I like studying a lot more since working with you. I want to be as smart as you someday. But I have to admit I like getting a practical education better than book learning. I see, though, that both are important."

"Yes, they are. You should look at everything as a learning experience, and as long as your sister is willing to teach you, you best let her."

"Yeah."

For the rest of the evening, Frank and Charlie concentrated on the work at hand.

That evening, after taking care of Pilot and eating his supper, Frank sat on what was shaping up to be his front porch, reflecting on the things he had learned about Grace—how she handled frustration, her interest in learning, her drive to be useful and of service. *It only makes me love her more. There, I said it. Yes, I'm ardently in love with Grace Saulsby.* It made him even more curious to know if he was always the cause of her foot stamping. *I'm sure my behavior this afternoon was the cause of it today. Charlie is a great kid and it's good that I'm getting to know him so well. I'm glad the Davies boy couldn't come to work with me. It may have hindered my opportunity to get to know Charlie. If things work out the way I want them to, I hope he will be ready to accept me into his family.*

Frank was not naive about how far he still had to go to make Grace his own, but his relationship with Charlie did give him comfort.

*****

Although still confused about her encounter with Frank, as she was organizing Charlie's assignment for the coming day, she reflected on the positive influence he was having on her brother and heaved a sigh. *Even if I've been mistaken about his interest in me, I have to be grateful for what he is doing for Charlie. Not only because Charlie has become an eager student, but the practical knowledge he's gaining will help him be more suited to live here. From what Charlie has told us, Frank's life is a lot different now than it was when he lived in Philadelphia. I should take a page out of his book and learn to be successful in the wild West.* She chuckled to herself at this reflection.

*****

Allen was aware, as Grace was finishing up her work for the day and getting his son's study material ready for the next, that in spite of the foot stamping, she had a calmness about her tonight that he hadn't noticed before and hoped it was an indication that she was coming to terms with living in Wylerton. Well, maybe she still would prefer to live elsewhere, but he could tell her depression about leaving Richmond was lifting. He was sure it had something to do with her interest in Frank Madison, although something had happened today. He thought better of asking.

23

The Midsummer Festival

There was less than a week left before the Midsummer Festival. Grace was sure it was different from anything she had experienced in Wylerton so far but kept forgetting to ask anyone about it, so one day she cornered Minnie in the mercantile who was looking at fabric.

"Minnie, please tell me about the Midsummer Festival."

"Well, it's the combination of an auction, dinner, and dance. We hold it in the Davieses' barn. The Davieses roast a calf over an open pit, the Blackburns bring cheese, and everyone else brings their own side dishes to complete the dinner. Most of the married ladies bring pies to share for dessert," she explained. "Each family brings something for the auction, like fruit from their trees, vegetables from their gardens, and things like that. The young boys go over to the Davies ranch a couple of days before and help them clean out their barn."

"Oh, is the dance formal?" asked Grace.

"Everyone dresses up," replied Minnie. "But it's not really formal."

"We don't have a garden," said Grace. "I don't know what I can bring."

"Didn't you tell me you pick strawberries and made jam?"

"Yes, I did."

"Then that's what you should bring and anything else you want to donate for the auction. The money is used to help the needy. That

126

quilt we made will bring a good price. You're a very good quilter, you know."

"Thanks, Minnie. My mother insisted I learn domestic skills. I hated it at the time but now I'm grateful for her wisdom. Are you going to make a dress for the festival out of that fabric you're looking at?"

"Yes," replied Minnie. "I haven't made a new dress in a long time. I could wear one of my old ones, but I like to sew."

"So do I," replied Grace.

They looked at the fabric together and discussed several options for Minnie's dress. Grace thought the satin she chose would make a lovely dress.

She considered buying herself fabric for a new dress but then she thought about the two ball gowns she had in her wardrobe and decided there was at least one she could alter to make it less formal. *I guess it was wise to bring a couple of ball gowns after all,* she thought on her way home.

Since there had been no evidence of social activities since they moved to Wylerton, Grace was looking forward to this summer festival. Other than church, she hadn't seen much of Frank since their encounter in the mercantile, so she hoped he would be at the festival and she could question him about his behavior.

*****

The day after helping get the Davieses' barn ready for the festival, Grace thought Charlie would be excited about going.

"Charlie, what are you going to wear to the festival tomorrow?" she asked, as he was gathering up his schoolwork.

"Oh, I'm not going."

"What?" said Grace. "After helping with the decorations and working so hard to clean out the barn, you're not going? Why?"

"I can't dance."

"Oh Charlie, I didn't think about that. I can teach you to dance. It's not really that hard, I promise."

"Are you sure?"

"Of course, I'm sure. Here, let's move the furniture back. I'll bet you can learn to waltz before Father gets home for supper tonight. The hardest part is learning to respond to the beat and rhythm of the music. "I'll hum the rhythm of a waltz, and you just sway to the beat."

Grace was glad Charlie picked up the timing to the music quickly. Two hours later after practicing the steps, they were able to move around the parlor together quite easily.

"Wow, I didn't think dancing would be so fun. I bet it will be even better when there is real music," Charlie said, grinning from ear to ear.

"Yes it will. I'm sure there are other dances neither of us know. We will just have to watch a couple of them and see if we can catch on," replied Grace, pleased that he had learned to waltz in such a short time. Charlie went off to work in a very happy mood.

Grace decided to wear her pale gold silk dress. She remembered Minnie had purchased satin for the dress she was going to make and Grace thought the silk would fit in just fine. After removing the cream-colored lace and brown bows from the skirt, she thought it plain enough to leave some lace on the bodice and the small bows on the sleeves. She was happy with the alterations and hoped she wouldn't look out of place. The gold was such a good color on her, and without the lace over skirt and just a sash around her waist, she was hopeful it didn't look too formal.

*****

The night of the festival it took Grace a long time to fix her hair. She struggled to keep the tears at bay. She and her mother had such wonderful chats when they were getting ready for social outings. Without any help, she couldn't quite get her hair exactly right. But when it was as close as she was sure she could get it, she decided to call it good. *It's in a barn after all.*

Charlie's mouth dropped open when he saw Grace finally come down the steps. Her father got a lump in his throat and fought to hold back the tears. It had been a long time since he'd seen Grace dressed so formally.

Her appearance reminded him so much of how exquisitely lovely his Charlotte was. He took a deep breath and wondered again if he'd made a mistake taking her away from Richmond, but he quickly compared Frank to Stuart and decided he was glad they were here.

Grace was pleased when she saw her father dressed in one of his usual business suits and Charlie wearing the new pants she made for him (that, thank goodness, still fit) with a white shirt and string tie. She thought they both looked very dashing.

"Do you think I'm dressed too formally, Father?" she inquired.

"I don't think you need to worry about it, daughter. No one is going to object to the way you look," he answered, without adding he thought she would most likely be the most beautiful young woman there.

They presented an elegant picture as they entered the barn. Perhaps a little more than elegant. Grace scanned the room to see if they were fitting in without realizing how breathtakingly beautiful she was. She had tied up her dark auburn hair with gold ribbons and the cut of her gown emphasized her long neck and the graceful lines of her shoulders. When they saw her, every man in the room stopped breathing. What Grace noticed was that, like her father, Mr. Jenkins was also wearing a suit. The dress that Minnie made was very attractive and that Priscilla's was very lacy. She let out a sigh of relief as their friends and neighbors greeted them. Not knowing what to expect, she had been in a nervous state all day. But now that they were here, she thought they were fitting in very nicely. She had no idea that most of the men in the room had never seen a woman as stunningly elegant as Grace in a ball gown that set off her beauty and figure to perfection.

The emotions that swelled in Frank's chest when he saw Grace enter the barn were painful. His heart started beating violently against his chest and his lungs lost their ability to take in air.

"Now there's one beautiful woman," said Willie who was standing next to him. "Never seen a woman that fit her name so perfectly. Ever noticed how she moves?"

Frank couldn't respond. He had never seen Grace, or any other woman for that matter, looking so magnificent. The gold gown swayed gently when she moved and with her hair piled on top of her head revealing the lines of her neck and shoulders, Frank, who already admired her beauty, could hardly believe what he was seeing. Along with all the other men in the barn, he, too, was breathless.

"Mind if I ask her to dance?"

"Willie, I don't have any claim on Miss Saulsby."

"Maybe not officially, but I saw the way you took off to rescue her from that rainstorm. *And*, I seen the way you always look at her. You definitely have a thing for that girl."

"You can ask her to dance" was all Frank could say.

He was struggling with an unfamiliar emotion. He had never known fear until it came to Grace Saulsby. When he decided to leave Philadelphia and face an unknown future, he was hopeful. When he faced death falling down the mountainside, he was resigned. As he moved West into new situations, he adapted. But when it came to Grace Saulsby, the prospect that she would not someday return his love and become his wife seized him with fear. Fear that without her his existence would cease to have meaning. With his heart pounding painfully in his chest, it was a struggle to keep his desire under control to go to her and gather her into his arms and confess his love and dire need for her. *When I do ask her to dance, will I be able to check my emotions?* He didn't have an answer. The more he saw of her the more he learned of her; the more he got to know her the more his admiration and love for her grew. He knew his heart and soul already belonged to her and only hoped the day would come when she would want to belong to him.

It didn't take Grace but a minute to spot Frank. Not only because he was tall but, as usual, she could sense his presence even in a barn full of people. He was dressed almost as formally as her father but without the jacket. She noticed he had trimmed his beard and his hair was cut much shorter. Grace decided he was almost handsome. She hoped he would ask her to dance. She needed to know why he had bolted from the mercantile and was determined to confront him about it.

When she saw Claire, Grace went to compliment her on her dress. She was sure it came from either New York or Paris.

"Claire, your dress is beautiful. I love the style."

"Thank you," responded Claire. She was glowing.

"Your dress is very pretty, too," said Claire. "It's one you brought from Virginia, isn't it?" Before Grace could reply, Mr. Jenkins was at their side.

"Hello, Mr. Jenkins," greeted Grace. "You are looking very handsome tonight."

"Thank you, Miss Saulsby, and you as well." Then he turned to Claire.

"I think you are the prettiest girl here," he whispered into her ear with a twinkle in his eyes.

Claire warmly smiled back and Grace was forgotten. It was so obvious they had eyes only for each other.

After the auction, when it came time to eat, everyone sat with their family or friends. Grace noticed that Frank was sitting with Willie Barton, Hank Wilder, and some of the other men from the mine. Charlie had mentioned that Hank was often helping Frank with his house. Grace thought he looked a little odd dressed up in a clean white shirt and clean pants. She was so used to seeing him without a shirt and wearing scruffy leather pants and his black apron. He was so muscular his shirt looked like a huge full sail. After dinner when the dancing started, he was the first one to ask her to dance. She liked Hank. He was a friendly, good-natured man. She wondered why he had never married and ventured to ask him about it while they were dancing, only to discover that he was a widower. Like her family, his wife and infant daughter had died from a fever. She was glad she could offer sincere sympathy.

Grace didn't lack for partners during the evening. She had to chuckle to herself when Willie Barton asked her to dance. *Is he just shy or is there something else going on?* He kept looking over at Frank. Most of the time, she, too, was able to keep her eyes on him. She noticed he danced with all the single ladies, young and old, and wondered why he didn't ask her. However, she was pleased to see Charlie following his example by asking Rosie Blackburn for a dance. Rosie was a cute girl, but like the other young girls her age, was at that awkward stage between girlhood and womanhood, too shy to feel comfortable in their own skin. But Charlie's example must have given the other young men courage because, after asking Rosie to dance, they followed suit, and from then on, none of the girls her age lacked for partners. She also noticed her father spending a good deal of time with Betty Packer. *I wonder if that's significant.*

Hard though it was to keep her mind off of Frank because she had been raised to be a lady, Grace made sure she gave her attention to each man that asked her to dance. As the evening progressed, she had the opportunity to dance with both of the Clarke brothers and still had a hard time figuring out what Minnie and Priscilla saw in them. But she was glad that both girls danced with each of the boys several times. She wondered why they thought they had to try so hard to attract them since they were both very pretty girls. She tried to remember when she was eighteen if that's the way she had acted. Then realized her mother's death had sobered her quite a bit.

Since Frank didn't make any attempt to dance with her, Grace concocted all kinds of scenarios about what she had done to push him away. *I scolded him when he carried me across the street. Hadn't we gotten past that? Maybe he's upset because I never sought him out to thank him for rescuing me from the rain, but surely he knew how embarrassed I had been. What is it I have done that has pushed him away? Has Charlie said something to discourage his interest? If he would only ask me to dance, I'm sure we could straighten things out.*

Frank kept his eyes on Grace the whole evening but, not trusting his emotions, didn't make any attempt to ask her to dance. He knew he had to wait for the sweetheart dance. As he watched, he noticed she graciously accepted every offer to dance, and then gave each partner her full attention. In his eyes this graciousness made her even more desirable. Toward the end of the evening, it was announced that the sweetheart dance was coming up and the men were told to grab their favorite gals. Grace was surprised to see Frank walking right toward her.

"May I?" he said, as he held out his hand.

She hesitated for a second, then put her hand in his. There it was again, the thrilling sensation that she felt every time he touched her and the fairy threads making it feel as if their hands were being woven together. It made her tighten her grip. Frank smiled. She didn't look at him for fear he would see how much he affected her. She had to catch her breath when he put his hand on her waist and she felt those invisible silk threads winding around it, tying his hand to her back. She was so caught in the whirl of this sensation that it took her a few minutes to realize that Frank was an excellent dancer. Not only because his movements were graceful but he was very skilled at leading, making it easy for her to follow. He drew her closer as they danced but he didn't speak to her. *This is no help. How am I going to find out what was wrong between us?* What she didn't realize was that, with his heart in his throat, Frank was having a hard time breathing, much less talking. And he was having a hard time waiting. He knew he was going to kiss her and hoped he could keep his desire for her under control so the kiss would be *gentlemanly*.

As the dance was ending, Grace decided to be blunt and just ask. She lifted her face to him just as the lanterns in the room were extinguished. Frank's lips were on hers. Her face was covered with his whiskers, but his smooth warm lips consumed all of her senses, igniting every nerve in her body. The touch of his lips was very gentle at first, then he slipped his fingers into the hair at the base of her neck and, for a second, deepened his kiss. Grace was caught up in the passion, and just as she realized she wanted to return the kiss, he pulled away. When his lips left hers, he whispered into her ear, "I didn't think I could keep from doing this in the mercantile. That's why I left so abruptly."

He pulled her tightly against him just as the lanterns were being relit. In that moment, all of her discontent was washed away and Grace felt at home in his strong embrace. Then his smoky blue eyes looked into her heart and, without another word, he was gone.

She stopped breathing. Her whole body was reeling from the experience of Frank Madison's kiss and embrace. *What just happened to me? That was not an ordinary kiss. He somehow made me part of him. I want to always feel his arms around me.* The realization washed over her like the wind before a storm, whipping through her and pressing against her very soul. *How has this happened? Do I even know him really?* Grace thought back over all the times she had been in Frank's presence. She had been drawn to him even before she knew his name. She remembered being able to feel him before she had even looked at him. *Is this kind of thing possible? I feel so connected to him. What's happening to me? Am I in love with him?* Grace couldn't shake these confusing thoughts. She stood there, dazed.

"Hey, sis, are you just going to stand there?" Charlie's voice brought her out of her trance. She mentally shook herself, and as they gathered up their things, she tried to act normally but her mind was reeling. *Does he love me? Does it mean that he isn't upset with me? Had he really left the mercantile to keep from kissing me? Is that what he said?*

Grace had a hard time sleeping that night. The memory of Frank's kiss made her smile. His absence left her feeling oddly insecure and lonely. She reflected again on their first encounters and knew from the very beginning she had been drawn to him. *Every time we meet I feel more and more tied to him.* How she craved his presence now. She drew her blankets up around her. They did nothing to alleviate her longing to feel the strength and warmth of Frank's arms. Her lips could still feel the tingling sensation caused by his kiss.

*****

The experience of kissing Grace was so profound, Frank started to ponder the strong feelings he'd had toward her even from the first time he had seen her. *I need her like I need air. I feel incomplete without her. I'm sure I'm in love with her, but is there something else about her that is causing all these overwhelming feelings?* After thinking back over all of his interactions with Grace, he realized he had known the first time he picked her up to carry her across the street that she seemed to belong to him. *No, it was even before that. It was probably the first time I followed her into the mercantile because I was drawn to her even then.* Now his whole body was aching for her. *I wonder how she responded to my kiss.* He knew it had surprised her. That when they announced the sweetheart dance, she probably hadn't realized what that meant. *I'm sure she didn't expect me to kiss her. Was she affected by it the same way I was? That was no ordinary kiss. I gave myself to her with that kiss. I should just talk to her. No, that might prove hard. I'm finding it harder and harder to maintain normal behavior around her. I've got to get a handle on my feelings or I'm going to scare her away and I can't let that happen.*

The Sunday after the festival, when Grace saw Frank in church, probably no one else could tell he was smiling at her, but the warmth in his eyes made her blush. As usual, Frank left immediately after the sermon. She was disappointed but was then taken by surprise when Roger Clarke approached her father requesting permission to court her. She and Claire were chatting nearby when she overheard the conversation.

"Mr. Saulsby, I would like to court your daughter," he said.

"I see," responded Allen. "Has Grace given you any indication that she would welcome your attention?"

"Well, no, but I'm sure she would."

"I'll tell you what, Mr. Clarke, when I have some evidence that Grace is interested, I'll get back to you with an answer. Until then, let's hold off. She is struggling to adjust to her life here in Wylerton. I don't want to place any burdens on her that I'm not sure she would welcome."

Roger Clarke wasn't happy with this answer but he knew he would have to concede. He bid Allen good day and left the church.

I wonder if he knows Minnie is crazy about him, thought Grace.

On the way home, Grace thanked her father for putting off Mr. Clarke. Her father didn't ask if there was anything was going on between her and Frank Madison, but Grace wondered if he knew.

24

Friendship

Grace was walking home from her father's office when she noticed three men riding toward the saloon. They looked hard and mean. It scared her when they smiled and tipped their hats at her, so she quickly turned away and walked into the mercantile.

"Hi, Mrs. Perkins," she said. "Did you see those men that just rode into town?"

"I didn't, Grace. Why, are they some people you know?"

"Heavens, no, Mrs. Perkins. They look like outlaws!"

"Oh goodness! I hope you're wrong. I read in the paper a few days ago that a train near Denver was robbed. I was hoping this country was getting too civilized for outlaws."

"Probably. But just in case, may I have a box of .45s, please, Mrs. Perkins."

"Certainly, dear. I surely hope you won't need them, but better safe than sorry."

When she was ready to leave, Grace looked out the window, and not seeing any strangers in the street, decided it was safe to walk home. The next day she got her father's gun out of one of the book chests, rounded up some old bottles and tin cans, and went out toward the river.

*****

Frank reached for his gun when he heard the first shot, but when two more followed, he realized someone was target shooting. He headed in the direction of the gunfire. It didn't take but a second to realize who it was. She wasn't wearing a bonnet and her dark auburn hair was shining in the sun. He felt his heart jump into his throat again—his typical reaction to the sight of Grace Saulsby. He reined Pilot to a stop and watched her for a minute. Even though she was doing everything wrong, she was beautiful to watch.

He slowly nudged Pilot forward, it not being wise to startle a novice with a gun in her hands.

As Grace reached down into her bucket of bullets, she heard a horse approaching, but before she looked up she knew who it was—the only person that affected her that way, Frank Madison. She was getting used to the way her heart reacted to him and the feel of those silken threads reaching out to connect her to him. She didn't understand why but she had become accustomed to the fact that this was always her physical response to him. She waited wondering what it would be like to be with him again. It had been several days but she was still reeling from the effect of his kiss. She had decided, if the opportunity ever arose, if he ever kissed her again, she would kiss him back, hoping she could get some control over the experience and not feel so undone and dominated like she did with their first kiss. *Silly girl, what makes you think he will kiss you again?* She realized she was desperately hoping he would.

Frank dismounted and dropped Pilot's reins on the ground knowing the horse wouldn't wander far.

"Miss Saulsby, why is a lady from Richmond target shooting?"

"Well, Mr. Madison, this isn't Richmond, and I saw some very unsavory-looking men in town yesterday. I thought it wise that I be prepared to defend myself."

"Yes, I noticed them, also. If you want to learn to use a gun, may I offer some help?"

"If you wish." The sound of his voice warmed her heart.

"First, if you are learning to shoot to defend yourself, you don't need to be so far away from your target." He picked up the bucket of bullets. Grace followed him as he drew within nine or ten feet of her targets.

"I don't understand how to aim the gun. I couldn't hit a single can," she complained.

"That's because you were aiming. What you should have been doing is pointing. Okay, try and hit one of the targets from this distance," he said, as he positioned himself behind her.

Grace raised the gun, but before she could pull the trigger, Frank said, "Stop. Now give me the gun and point your finger at the target." She did.

"What do you notice about the difference between aiming the gun and pointing your finger?"

"My arm is more relaxed and I'm not holding it as high without the gun."

"Exactly. One of the steps to learning to use a gun is to keep your arm relaxed."

"But the gun is heavy."

"You can still learn to hold your arm in a relaxed way. This will also help your arm to absorb the kick without knocking you off balance."

He handed her the gun.

"Okay, point the gun at a can."

As she did, Frank, from his position behind her, put his hands on her shoulders. She sucked in air and stopped breathing.

"Keep your shoulders relaxed," he instructed.

Doesn't he realize I can't relax when he touches me? When he released his hold, she took a deep breath and tried to relax her shoulders.

"Now just point at the target and pull the trigger."

This time she hit the target, but the kick of the gun forced her back against Frank. He put his hands on her upper arms to steady her. Her heart was racing.

"That was really good. Now you need to learn how to do that without losing your balance. It's very important when defending yourself against someone who is skilled with a gun to look as if you are, too. Shooting a human being is a lot different than shooting at a target. A person familiar with killing knows that and will not be intimidated by an amateur, so it's important that your body language doesn't show either fear or inexperience. And, Grace," he said, as he tightened his grip on her arms, "If you really need to defend yourself, you must pull the trigger before they get within arm's length. If the gun is snatched out of your hand, it can't help you. Do you understand?"

"Yes."

"Promise me," he demanded as he increased the pressure of his grip.

"I promise," she said, feeling the urgency in his demand.

Frank let go of her arms and took a step back.

Grace was almost undone by the thrill that surged through her when he addressed her by her given name. He didn't seem to notice what he had done because he continued to bark out instructions.

"Now strengthen your stance. Move your feet a little further apart. Hold the gun a little lower with a bend in your elbow. Point at another can and pull the trigger," he commanded. "You need to control the kick of the gun, but don't fight it."

"Right," said Grace, saluting and clicking her heels as she imitated his military voice, "feet apart, shoulders relaxed, elbow bent."

Frank chuckled. "Did I really sound like that?" he inquired.

"A little," she answered, smiling.

"Sorry," he said, realizing his rough demanding voice was an effort to tap down the emotional rush he felt when he touched Grace and the anxiety he felt at her ever being in danger.

Grace followed his instructions but missed the can. However, she didn't get quite as thrown off balance.

"That's very good," he praised with a smile in his voice. "Try again. Remember, you want just your arm to absorb the kick."

"Yes, sir," she answered with a giggle.

This time the bullet hit really close to the target and Grace kept her balance. She was so excited she whirled around toward him her smile radiant, her eyes shining. Frank grabbed her wrist. In her excitement, she almost slammed the gun into his chest.

Their eyes met. His arms went around her waist and he pulled her close, giving into his desire to really hold her. The fairy threads were whirling around her heart so fast Grace felt as if they were being completely wrapped together. She recognized the feeling of safety and protection that was always present when she was in his arms and suddenly wished it was where she could stay forever. It dawned on her she was no longer afraid of whatever it was that was making her feel as though she belonged to this man. The gun fell into the grass. Frank couldn't keep his hands out of her hair. It felt as exquisite as it looked. He buried his face in its luxurious softness, then tightening his hold, pulled her head back. His mouth captured hers. This time when he didn't pull away, Grace returned his kiss. They were at home in their embrace and sharing the same passion. The thick soft feel of her hair was almost as delicious as her lips. A thought flashed through his mind, *Heaven couldn't be better than this.*

Their kisses became heated. Frank was the first one to come to his senses. He realized the need to check his desire. When he broke the seal of their kiss, he pulled her even tighter against him. Then realizing the need to make her part of himself was probably causing her pain, he took a deep breath and released her.

"I'm sorry, I shouldn't have done that," he said. "I should go." Then he looked at her and saw the longing in her eyes, her beautiful disheveled hair falling over her shoulders. He pulled her into his arms again. His embrace was even more crushing this time. Grace couldn't breathe, but she never wanted to be anywhere else. "Grace," he whispered. His voice husky and full of need. Then he released her again. "I really must go, I know my behavior is inappropriate. Forgive me," he said and walked away.

She stood there watching him go. She couldn't understand why he was leaving. *He must be sharing my feelings.* The experience answered the questions of his effect on her. The puzzlement of why she had always felt secure in his arms. Why she had always been drawn to him. *I belong to Frank Madison. I hardly know him, really, but for some reason I belong to him. Why is he walking away? I've never been kissed like that. I've never kissed anyone like that. Can't he tell I love him?* Dazed by this realization and the residual sensation of his embrace and kisses, Grace could neither move nor speak, so she just stood there watching him mount his horse and ride away. She tried to reign in her emotions and think of some reason why he was leaving when she so desperately wanted to still be kissing him. The idea of propriety flitted across her mind but was quickly dismissed. What did she care for propriety? She just wanted to be in Frank's arms. Her heart ached as the distance between them increased. *I want to always be with him. I hope he will remember his promise to show me the country around here. It would be wonderful to ride with him. Doing anything with him would be wonderful.* She watched Frank until he was almost out of sight. She felt abandoned. *I've had this feeling before. Every time he leaves me, actually. Can it be true that I actually belong to him in some way?* When he was out of sight, she picked up the gun and fired at one of the targets and missed. It took several more shots to put into practice all of Frank's instructions, but it felt good when she was successful. It made her feel close to him and the noise and energy of shooting the gun helped settle her emotions.

Frank heard Grace's gun fire and wished he could watch her, but he didn't dare even turn and look at her as he rode away. His emotions were raging with desire. She was a proper Southern lady. He hadn't even spoken to her father about courting her and he was concerned at his wanton need to have her. *She responded to my kisses. We are just getting acquainted and haven't even talked about what's going on between us. I hope what just happened didn't overwhelm her. She needs to be a part of my life. Should I have just confessed I love her? No, not the right circumstances or the right time. We were alone, and my desires were almost running out of control.* Still, worried about what Grace thought about what just happened between them, he prayed her feelings for him in some way matched his. *I will go about this in the proper way. I'll ask for permission to court her.*

*****

The next day, when Frank saw Grace's father going into the cafe, he followed him in.

"May I sit with you, sir?" he asked.

"Certainly," responded Allen.

141

"I'd like permission to court your daughter, Mr. Saulsby," said Frank.

"That doesn't come as much of a surprise, son," smiled Allen. "The way you look at her hasn't been lost on me, but I have a suggestion. Let's keep the agreement informal. I think Grace is still struggling with living in the West and might still harbor the idea that she will someday go back to Richmond. Because of that, she might resist a formal courtship."

"I see," said Frank, not willing to reveal the passionate kisses they'd exchanged.

"Just continue building your friendship with her," Allen encouraged.

"Oh, of course," smiled Frank. "I understand what you are saying." *There is wisdom in his suggestion, but I wonder what he would say if he had seen the way she kissed me yesterday?*

*****

Friday night when it was growing too dark to work, knowing that the boy didn't have to study on Saturday, he asked Charlie if he would like to go riding the next day.

"Wow, are you kidding?" he responded. "That would be the greatest."

Frank was glad Charlie had taken as much interest in his horses as he hoped he would.

"I spoke to your sister once about showing her around the country. Do you think she would like to join us?"

"Yeah," Charlie answered. "I think she has been making a split skirt so she would be able to ride with a regular saddle and she got some riding boots. She was talking to me once how none of the women out here use sidesaddles like they did in Richmond. Maybe she is planning to ask our father to buy some horses. Do you want me to ask her?"

"Yes," said Frank. "That would be appreciated."

He realized it would mean losing a good part of, or perhaps a whole day, he usually spent on the house, but spending time with

Grace would be worth it. Spending time with Grace was fast becoming a necessary part of his well-being.

Saturday morning Frank was pleased to see both Charlie and Grace walking toward his corral. The joy that swelled up in him was indescribable. He'd saddled all three horses, just in case. But at the time, he was less than hopeful. Now his heart was racing and he felt like jumping up and down like a schoolboy.

"I'm glad you could both come," he said, as they drew near. "We should be able to get in a good ride before it gets too hot."

"You bought the horse with the white sock," said Grace. "It was at the stables so long I began to think there was something wrong with her," she remarked as she began to pat the horse's neck and talk to her.

"No," answered Frank. "I needed to keep them at the livery until I got my corral built. I had to pay Mr. Nelson a pretty penny for her because she is such a fine animal."

"Oh, but you were able to buy her in spite of the price?"

"Well, yes," answered Frank. "I named her Tabby. She has some spirit, but she also has a loving personality. I plan to breed horses, and Pilot, Tabby, and Gray here are the start of my herd. Gray looks a bit beat up so Mr. Nelson was selling her cheap, but I could tell she's a strong healthy animal even though she looks a bit rough on the outside."

Like you, thought Grace.

"Hey, let's get going," said Charlie impatiently. "I guess I'm riding Gray."

"Yes, you are," said Frank, smiling.

"You should know," said Grace, "I have never ridden astride."

"Yes, Charlie mentioned something to that effect. I think you will actually find it easier," responded Frank. "I'll have you ride around in the corral for a while to get a feel for it." He showed her how to put her left foot in the stirrup while grabbing the horn and swing her right leg over the horse. Since Grace was tall, she could have managed on her own, but Frank instinctively put his hands on her waist as she attempted to mount. She hesitated. She hoped he would think her timid about the task, but it was the thrill his touch sent through her body that distracted her. She took a deep breath, then swung herself into the saddle. She liked the security she felt sitting astride. *Much more natural than a sidesaddle.* It didn't take but a couple of turns around the corral before she could say, "Okay, I think I'm ready."

Unlike Charlie who had ridden around the countryside with the Davies boy, other than going across the river to pick strawberries, this was Grace's first time outside of town. As Frank led them toward the river, she was amazed at the beauty of the country. The grass they were riding through was blowing in waves across the meadow. She was familiar with walking through this kind of grass, but sitting on a horse was an entirely different sensation. It gave her the feeling of traveling through water. It was a fascinating experience.

Frank took them upstream along the river, and then onto the trail that led into the high meadow. Grace was a bit nervous riding up the steep terrain. She had never ridden anywhere but on flat level ground. She clung onto the horn. *Now I know why the women here ride astride. I would have trouble staying on this horse in a sidesaddle.* They then went across the meadow and up a narrow trail that led to a plateau with an outlook where they could see across the rolling hills of the valley. Frank didn't mention they were on his land. He wanted Grace to come to admire the area without being distracted by its connection to him.

"Why, this is magnificent," said Grace. "I never imagined this rugged open country could be so amazing. It's thrilling to be able to look out and see so much of the landscape all at once. Its breathtaking, isn't it?"

"Yes," responded Frank, but he wasn't looking at the view.

"This place is so different from Virginia, I was afraid to venture away from town not realizing what I was missing."

"It is very different from the East, but it has its own beauty," said Frank. "I have the feeling it won't stay this pristine for long as more people discover its unique qualities. I'm glad I came out here at a time when the land could still be bought cheap."

"Were you buying land the day I saw you in my father's office?"

"I was," he answered but didn't expand on her question.

"My father thinks, like you, that more people will be moving into the area. I suppose the two silver mines are doing well."

"They are," answered Frank. "But I think people will move here for other reasons. The Davieses have found it great country for raising cattle. I hope to have similar success raising horses. And the Blackburn's dairy farm is doing well. The cheese they make is very much in demand in Denver. The Clarkes are being smart about reseeding the areas they log. I suspect their business will also continue to grow as the area gets settled. So far, the people who have settled here have found this to be good country."

"Yes," responded Grace. "My father has received notification of forty-five hundred acres of homesteading land. If they are as fortunate as the people already here, I suspect they will think that, too." This conversation made Grace look at the country around her with new eyes. The beautiful horse farms in Virginia were small compared to how many horses a person could raise in country like this. She wondered if some of the land they were looking at belonged to Frank but didn't ask.

Just after noon, they stopped to eat the food Grace had thoughtfully packed.

"These fried potato slices are the best I've ever tasted," remarked Frank.

"When my mother insisted I learn to cook, I discovered I liked experimenting with spices and herbs. They are seasoned with a mixture I created."

"Yeah, and you should taste her fried chicken," piped in Charlie. "That's my favorite."

"And the dried beef strips?" questioned Frank.

"Ginger and maple syrup," said Grace

"Grace is a really good cook," said Charlie.

"Yes, I can see that," said Frank.

While they were eating, Frank explained the terrain and the different kinds of vegetation. Both she and Charlie were impressed with how much he knew about the area and its history, and Grace enjoyed the banter between Charlie and Frank about the work on the house.

She and Frank shared their feelings about the loss of their families, realizing they had some similar reactions. However, she came to see that even though Frank had been profoundly affected by the loss of his family, he was healing and moving on with his life. Frank's vitality and enthusiasm about the future lifted her spirits. She decided she needed to do a better job of accepting her new circumstances. As the day progressed and she got to know him better, she began to see why he was so well-liked, and perhaps why she was so drawn to him. There was a feeling of warmth and kindness that radiated from him and an optimism that made her feel hopeful about life. She was determined to improve those attributes in herself and became aware that she very much wanted to be the kind of person he would admire.

"I found a plant on our property that smells like sage. However, I'm not sure it's edible. I use sage in my seasoning mixes, but I've never seen the actual plant. I've been concerned about what to do when my mixes are depleted. Mr. Perkins sells a few spices and herbs, but their freshness is sometimes questionable. It would be interesting to work with fresh plants. I'm sure there must be some kinds of herbs growing in the area. Do you know where I can find them?" asked Grace.

"I don't," responded Frank. "But there is an Indian village about ten miles west of here. I've talked to the medicine man several times when he's been in town so I know he speaks English. He is very friendly, and I'm sure he can help answer that question. If we start out at dawn next week, I think we can make the trip in one day. It will make for a long day, but it might be worth it."

"I would like that very much," responded Grace.

"Next Saturday morning, then?" asked Frank.

"Yes, let's plan on it," agreed Grace.

It was fairly late in the afternoon as they were nearing Frank's corral. Grace said, "I had no idea when we started out this morning how wonderful this country is. Thank you so much for this day."

"I hope it is the first of many," responded Frank. "I keep the saddles in the barn. You and Charlie are welcome to come over and ride the horses anytime."

"If you were wise you wouldn't make that offer to Charlie. That boy is addicted to riding."

"That's not fair, sis," complained Charlie. "I wouldn't ride more than once a day."

"Once a day all day," said Grace smiling at Frank.

"I can see I need to rephrase that offer. Charlie, you may ride Gray for an hour after you finish your studies and any chores you need to do for your sister. And I expect you to be ready to work at our scheduled time."

Charlie was about to whine, but the look on his sister's face made him change his mind.

"I guess that's fair," he said reluctantly.

After several hours of riding in a way she wasn't used to, Grace said she preferred to walk back to their house.

They each took the saddles off and rubbed down their horses. As Frank was walking them home, he asked Grace what color she thought he should paint his house.

"Well," she responded. "Since your barn is dark red, you should paint your house that same color. That way, they will look as if they belong together. Of course, you don't need to use quite as much red on the house. A lot of white trim would look good, like around the windows and the porch and fascia. Just paint the outside walls the same color as the barn. Everything else white. Perhaps the actual windows would look good black or a very dark gray. Yes, I think adding a third color would be nice."

"Thank you, that sounds like an excellent idea. I'm glad I asked for your advice." Frank smiled to himself. Their friendship was growing, but he was sure Grace didn't have any idea he was planning the house with her in mind.

"Until next Saturday, then," nodded Frank as he dropped them off.

"Yes, thank you," said Grace and Charlie in unison. Because the day was mostly spent, Frank excused Charlie from working. It occurred to Grace that he had sacrificed time he could have been working on his house. It added to her admiration of him and the pleasure she felt about their day together. She was grateful for it and the opportunity of getting to know him better.

That night, as Grace lay in bed reflecting on the day, she realized she had not only fallen in love with the country but she knew she was totally in love with Frank Madison. She recognized how comfortable she was in his company now. The sound of his voice was like the morning sun, gentle and warm, and she loved his slight Northern accent. Every part of her wanted to belong to him. She thought about the times he had kissed her. His kisses and his embrace stirred up emotions she had never experienced. They were delicious. She wondered what he would look like without his beard but knew it didn't matter. She realized that her attraction to him was connected to something deeper than his physical appearance. Yet she had to admit that she craved his touch. *My very soul wants to be connected to him, if that's possible,* she thought, hoping Frank was developing similar feelings for her.

That night, Frank reflected on the wisdom of getting to know Grace better. *It was the right thing to do. I don't know how it is that I was in love with her before I even knew her. Now I'm hopelessly besotted.* He thought back on the first day he saw her, realizing again that even then he was instantly drawn to her. *Did we know each other in a former life?* he fantasized, still not quite able to put his finger on why he was sure he and Grace were meant to be together. He wondered on more than one occasion about the possibility of Grace being his mystery girl in Richmond. He didn't know the answer, but he knew he and Grace had a special connection and couldn't imagine spending his life with anyone but her.

*****

The next Saturday Frank showed up at the Saulsbys before sunrise, with Tabby and Gray saddled and ready to go. When Grace was so eager to be spending the whole day with Frank, Charlie began to suspect something was going on between them. He wondered if it was more than discovering where to find herbs that had his sister so eagerly looking forward to the day.

As they drew near the Indian encampment, Grace began to feel a little nervous. This was so different from the drawings of the Native villages she had seen in books when she and Caroline were studying together. This was real, and, having never visited people of a different culture, she didn't know what to expect. Now here she was going to visit people who many thought of as savages. As they got close to the Indian settlement, she smelled meat cooking, and saw a woman carrying water from the nearby creek. She heard children playing. The happy voices of the children did much to settle her uneasiness. Frank dismounted and took off his gun belt.

"Stay here," he instructed. "I'll see if Black Feather is around. They are often out hunting this time of year." He handed Charlie Pilot's reins and walked into the camp. When the children noticed Grace and Charlie sitting on their horses on the edge of the camp, they were curious about the people with white faces in their village and came over to inspect them. Grace smiled and said hello, but it made them run away.

"Maybe they think we're ghosts with our pale skin," chuckled Charlie.

A few minutes later, Frank came back with a smile on his face.

"We're in luck," he said. "Black Feather is here and said we are welcome to come into his tepee." He reached up to help Grace dismount. His touch made her feel safe, as it always did, and she began to look forward to this new experience with less trepidation.

The Indian standing by the tepee had graying hair, but he looked very strong. His muscles were well formed and, although his face was lined with wrinkles and he was missing a couple of teeth, he was quite handsome. Grace felt a little shy looking at his almost naked body. As they entered the tepee, she was surprised at how roomy it was. The ground was covered with the most colorful blankets she had ever seen. Black Feather indicated where they should sit and asked, "So you are interested in learning about edible plants?"

"Yes," answered Grace. "When my mother taught me how to cook, I became interested in how spices and herbs affect the flavor of food and began to make my own seasoning mixes. I brought a lot with me when we moved from Virginia, but I know they won't last forever. All the spices and herbs I use came in tins. I have no idea what the actual plants look like and I'm hoping many of the ones

I'm familiar with grow around here, and I wouldn't be surprised if there are some native to this area that I'm not familiar with. Mr. Madison thought perhaps you could teach me to recognize the plants and where to find them."

"Let's walk," he answered.

Black Father took them several yards from the village and stopped next to a bush with silver gray leaves. He reached down, picked some of the leaves, rubbed them between his fingers, and smelled them.

He indicated to Grace to do the same.

"Sage. I use this all the time, and we actually have some plants like this on our property but didn't know if it was the same kind of sage we eat."

"If the sage on your property looks similar to this, it is edible. But there is another kind of wild sage that is not," said Black Feather.

"We use it for medicine, but it's not good for food," he explained. "Make sure the plant on your property looks like this one." They wandered down closer to the creek, and Black Feather stopped by a small bush with fluffy white flowers. He indicated they should pick some and smell it.

"Celery?" questioned Grace.

"That's not what we call it," responded Black Feather. "We use it on rabbit meat."

"Wish I'd known that when I was traveling from the East Coast," said Frank. "I'll bet it would have helped make all those rabbits I ate taste better."

"You actually ate rabbits?" questioned Charlie, as he scrunched up his nose.

"Better than starving," smiled Frank, deciding not to mention eating snake meat.

Black Feather showed them some wild onion and told her to look for it near the riverbanks. Then he showed her a juniper plant and told her where to find it and what foods to use it on. On the way back to their horses, he stopped by a somewhat scraggly-looking plant and pulled it up by the roots. After brushing it off, he pulled out his knife, cut off a piece of the root, and handed it to Grace. She smelled it. "Sarsaparilla! I've made sarsaparilla tea but, again, didn't have any idea what the plant looked like. Will you let us come again? I'm sure there is much more I need to learn," she said, as she was putting the plants they had collected into her saddlebag.

"We are out hunting most of the time, but the next time I come into town, I'll make arrangements with Frank for us to meet again."

"Oh, I would like that so much," responded Grace.

On the ride home, Grace chatted enthusiastically about all that she had learned and how she was looking forward to working with fresh herbs and creating new seasoning mixes.

"I wonder if I could start an herb garden so I wouldn't have to ride all over the country looking for them."

"I'm sure if they grow in the area you could raise them in a garden," responded Frank. "If it's something you enjoy doing, why don't you think about selling your spice mixes in the Perkins Mercantile? I think Mrs. Perkins would love to sell them, and since there would be no shipping cost, she could probably sell them at a reasonable price."

"That's an interesting thought," answered Grace. "I would need to experiment first. Some of these herbs, like juniper, are unfamiliar to me, but I like the idea."

Frank remembered Charlie telling him about Grace liking a challenge and was glad he had suggested something she seemed excited about.

That night Charlie watched Frank and his sister as he was rubbing down Gray. He noticed how cheerful Grace was in Frank's company. He watched Frank dismount first and take Tabby's reins, as Grace dismounted. They were standing very close, and Grace brushed against him. Neither moved for several minutes. Because every muscle in Frank's body had gone ridged in his effort to keep from putting his arms around Grace, he was holding very still. She was trying to catch her breath at the thrill of his touch. *That's odd,* thought Charlie, as he watched them standing like statues. Then he noticed that they kept looking at each other as they were rubbing down their horses. It occurred to him that he would really like it if Frank married his sister.

"Frank," said Charlie, as they were walking home, "Why don't you sit with us in church tomorrow?"

Frank was a bit taken aback by this invitation. He would like nothing better than to sit for a whole hour next to Grace. He also knew it would be paramount to announcing an engagement which is exactly what happened the first time Mr. Jenkins sat with the Johnsons. Of course, it wasn't many days later that his engagement to Claire Johnson was announced. He hoped that day would come for him. Yes, he would sit next to Grace in church someday, but tomorrow wasn't that day.

"Well, thank you for that invitation, Charlie," said Frank. "But you know I sit with Hank and Willie. I wouldn't want to hurt their feelings now, would I?"

"I suppose not," responded Charlie, disappointed. Grace smiled.

Little did Charlie realize the turmoil his suggestion caused in her heart. The thought of spending that much time touching Frank both thrilled and frightened her. When she brushed up against him as she was dismounting, it sent such a thrill through her she was paralyzed. The silk threads were wrapping around her heart so tightly she was afraid it might stop beating, and she wanted so much to have his arms wrapping around her, also. She didn't know how long they stood together before Tabby pulled at the reins, causing Frank to move away. She just knew she craved the feel of his touch. *Did Charlie see us standing together like a couple of wooden Indians?* she thought. *I suppose he's getting old enough to see there is something going on between us. Maybe I should at least let him know I like Frank.* As she pondered this and her impatience about having to wait a week before spending another day with him, a definite decision came to mind. She would start talking to her father and Charlie about her interest in Frank.

25

Charlie's Rescue

Grace was peeling potatoes and gazing out the kitchen window when she saw Frank galloping across the field with Tabby and Gray in tow. Since it wasn't Saturday, she knew something must be wrong. She rinsed off her hands and stepped outside. When he got to the steps, he said, "Charlie must have come over at the usual time to ride Gray. But when I got to the house, she was standing by the corral with her saddle on and a bleeding knee, but there is no sign of Charlie."

"I'll grab my medical bag and be right back." With anxiety raging in her chest, Grace snatched off her apron as she ran to get the kit and was back in less than a minute, not taking the time to put on her riding skirt. Frank drew Tabby up alongside the step so Grace could mount from there.

"How are we going to find him?" Grace asked, as she threw herself onto the saddle. "Do you know where he goes?"

"I'm not sure, but I'm hoping Gray here will lead us to him," he said, as he wound the horse's reins around her saddle horn.

When Grace was settled in the saddle, Frank gave Gray a pat on her backside.

"Okay, girl," he said. "Show us where he is."

To their surprise, Gray took off at a dead run. Frank and Grace followed suit across the meadow to the river where she led them along the river to the trail that went up to the high meadow. Crossing the meadow, the horse started up another narrow trail on a rocky cliff but stopped when she came to a place where the rocks were loose. Frank dismounted and, leaving Pilot standing next to Gray, started walking up ahead. Grace followed suit, tying Tabby's reins to a nearby bush. It wasn't long before Frank spotted Charlie lying on the ground.

Grace, following Frank, saw Charlie about the same time. "Charlie!" she screamed, as she rushed over and threw herself on the ground next to him, just as Frank was putting his face next to Charlie's nose.

"He is breathing," he assured her. "But let's check for injuries before we move him," he cautioned.

They started feeling his arms and legs and, not finding anything unusual, Frank gently turned his head. That's when they discovered the blood and a bump the size of a walnut.

"Charlie, Charlie," Grace cried, trying to bring him back to consciousness.

"Gray stumbled and I fell" was all he could say before blacking out again. As she was getting some gauze and Mercurochrome to clean the wound, Frank suddenly stood, whipped the gun out of his holster, and fired. Grace gave a startled cry. The bullet hit the ground near the animal's feet, and the mountain lion ran off just as Frank hoped it would.

Wide-eyed, Grace asked, "How did you know it was there?"

"I heard it approach," he responded.

"You heard it approach?" she questioned incredulously. "It didn't make any noise."

"It did, actually," answered Frank, smiling. "Listening to the sounds around me is a survival skill I perfected traveling across the country. I most likely wouldn't have made it this far without it."

Grace stared at him in wonder. *Can this man get any more interesting?*

Returning her attention back to her brother, after applying the Mercurochrome, Grace wrapped a bandage around his head to cover the wound.

"How are we going to get him home?" she questioned. Frank could hear the worried desperation in her voice. His response was tender but definite.

"I'm going to pick Charlie up and carry him back down to the horses," he said. "The trick will be to get Pilot to stand still when I'm trying to mount holding Charlie. It won't feel right and he might baulk. You will need to keep him steady."

Frank gently picked Charlie up and carefully walked back down the trail to where they'd left the horses. Grace took a hold of Pilot's reins close to his bit with one hand and grabbed onto the saddle horn with the other, while Frank, holding Charlie close to his chest, put his foot in the stirrup. Pilot started skidding away, but Grace put her face close to his ear and talked to him. Her firm grip and the distraction worked, and Frank was able to get Charlie and himself into the saddle.

"You're going to have to lead us past this area of loose rocks," he said. "I think I better keep Charlie as still as possible in case he has some internal injuries we haven't detected. Leave the other two horses here and walk Pilot down this steep terrain," he instructed. "When we get to more level ground past these rocks, tie him to something and come back for the other horses. After that, I think we should be fine."

"Okay," responded Grace. She said a silent prayer that she could get them successfully past the steep narrow area that led to the meadow and that Frank would be able to stay in the saddle while carrying her brother. She talked to Pilot as she started down the trail, explaining the situation and asking him to understand. It seemed to work. Once they got to more level ground, she tied Pilot to a scrub tree and he stood very still. Then she went back for the other horses. *She does have a way with horses. I guess I shouldn't be surprised. She's good at so many things,* reflected Frank, as he waited for Grace to return. Knowing her trepidation would be great, he thought how levelheaded she was being through this whole ordeal. *Amazing girl.*

When she returned to where they'd left Tabby and Gray, instead of mounting Tabby, she grabbed both their reins and walked them past the rocky incline. When she got back to where she left Frank and Pilot, she also took ahold of Pilot's reins. Frank said, "Just lead Pilot. Don't try to lead Gray."

"Do you think she will follow us?"

"Yes," he answered.

Grace kept ahold of Pilot's reins as she mounted Tabby. She was sure, because of the extra weight and because she was holding onto his reins, that Pilot knew there was something unusual going on, but she was glad that he was willing to cooperate and match Tabby's gait as they slowly walked back home. She was also impressed that Frank was correct in his confidence that Gray would follow.

When they got back to the house, Grace maneuvered Pilot next to the porch so Frank could dismount more easily. She directed Frank up to Charlie's bedroom where he laid him carefully on his bed. He still had not regained consciousness. Grace threw herself on her knees and took Charlie's hand in hers. When Frank saw the tear fall on her hands, he knelt beside her.

"Dear Lord," she prayed, "Please don't take Charlie like you did mother and James. I don't know if Father and I could recover from such a loss."

Frank's heart went out to Grace, and he instinctively put his arms around her and pulled her into a firm embrace. She didn't pull away. He could feel his shirt getting wet as she pressed her face against his chest. A turmoil of emotions was whirling around inside him—concern for Charlie, sympathy for Grace's anxiety, the joy of having her in his arms, in addition to a desire to make everything all right. He didn't know how long they knelt together.

A groan from Charlie intruded.

"Please fetch me some water, will you Frank?" requested Grace, pulling away to give Charlie her attention.

"Of course." He stood up and left the room.

Grace lifted the bandage and carefully tried to move Charlie's hair away from the lump on his head. The blood had dried in his matted hair so she couldn't see the condition of the wound. When Frank got back with the water, she retrieved a clean washcloth from the bottom draw of the wardrobe, removed the bandage, and wiped the area clean. As she inspected it more closely, it didn't look deep and she determined he wouldn't need stitches. It was just a surface cut. However, she was not relieved. The area was still swelling. That meant the injury might be internal. Not a good thing.

"I wish there was a real doctor here," she sighed.

"Let's just watch him for a few more hours," responded Frank. "If, at any point, things get really worse, we can take him to Denver. I'll go to the livery right now and see about setting up one of the wagons so it will ride smoother."

"Thank you, Frank. Help me get his boots and clothes off first, will you?" she requested.

He helped her pull off Charlie's boots and pants. When they removed his shirt, they discovered a scrape on his elbow but it was nothing serious. After they got him comfortably settled in bed, Frank turned to leave.

"Oh, Frank, I can't thank you enough. Charlie might be dead, if not for you. How will we ever repay you?"

"You don't need to even think about repaying me. I'm very fond of Charlie, and I promised the people who saved my life that one day I would do the same for someone else. Besides, I have a strong feeling your prayer will be answered."

Grace smiled at him, took a step closer, and gave him a firm hug. It warmed his heart, and he longed to never let her go, but that would be selfish when Charlie's needs were so pressing. When Grace declined any further assistance, he left.

"Please let my father know what's happened, will you?" she called down the steps, just as Frank was crossing the parlor.

"Of course," he called back. "I'll take Tabby into town so your father can ride her back. You can leave her here in case you need her."

"Thank you very much. That will be wonderful."

It seemed so natural to be with Frank now. Over the past two weeks, their Saturday outings were breaking down the awkwardness that existed when they were first getting acquainted. Grace was pondering how acutely she was feeling his absence as she was sitting by Charlie's bed. *It was because I had such an unusual reaction to him right from the first moment I looked at him. No, even before I looked at him. Just his presence in the mercantile that day had an effect on me. Something has been drawing me to him right from the start, and every time we meet, I feel more and more attached to him. Getting to know him has only strengthened those feelings.*

She felt Charlie's head as these thoughts were running through her mind. It was too warm. She prayed again as she was getting some clean water to put a cold washcloth on his head.

A few minutes later, her father came home.

"How's my son?" he asked, as he came bounding into the room. Grace recognized the worried expression on his face. She had seen it before. She stood up and gave her father a hug.

"He has to be all right, Father," she sobbed. "We just can't lose him, too."

Allen Saulsby stood very still. He was almost paralyzed with fear. Concern for Charlie and his ability to handle losing another family member was almost more than he could handle. He, too, knelt by Charlie's bed and prayed.

That night was agony. Charlie's fever got worse. He would wake up occasionally but couldn't stay conscious for more than a few minutes. Grace and her father took turns tending him through the night. They forced him to drink water every few hours. Sometimes he almost regained consciousness, but it was a night of great anxiety for Grace and her father. They were torn between keeping him still and taking him to a doctor in Denver. His condition wasn't good, but moving him just didn't feel right. Then early the next morning, his fever broke. The swelling wasn't getting any worse, but neither Grace nor her father knew if that was a good thing or a bad.

The next day, Frank sat down with Allen in the cafe.

"How is Charlie doing? Since you are here, does that mean his condition has improved?" he asked.

"His fever broke last night, but he can't stay conscious for more than a few minutes at a time. I came into work to keep myself busy and take my mind off the worry. There is nothing for me to do at home but wait."

"Well, my offer still stands if you decide you want to take him to Denver."

"Thanks, Frank. It's such a hard decision. What if the jarring of the trip would cause further damage? Grace is beside herself. I am, too, actually."

"I'll come around after work to see if you need anything," responded Frank.

Betty pulled Frank aside when Allen left. "Please stop by tonight before you go out to the Saulsby place, Frank. I've some got some rolls and soup I want you to take to them."

"Of course, Betty. I'd be happy to do that."

That night, when he dropped off the rolls and soup, Frank noticed the woodpile was almost depleted. There was enough wood for summer cooking but not nearly enough for winter. The next day, Frank made arrangements to have Rich Davies haul wood from the shed he'd build, glad he'd kept it well stocked after Elvira passed away. He wanted to ensure that the Saulsbys would have plenty of wood for the winter.

Betty herself came by on the third day. She informed them that on Sunday the reverend asked everyone to pray for Charlie. Then Beth Ann Perkins came by with a remedy *guaranteed to cure whatever ails you.* Grace and Allen were willing to try anything.

On the fourth day, Charlie regained consciousness long enough to take beef broth and get down to the outhouse. He didn't have any memory loss and gave coherent answers to their questions. He went right back to sleep, however, but both Grace and her father were breathing easier.

Charlie gradually got better. He had no signs of a damaged brain. No internal injuries were ever manifested. The townspeople who had been offering prayers shared the joy in this blessing to the Saulsby family. Two weeks after his accident, Charlie was complaining about having to study when Frank was so far behind in building his house in spite of the fact that he had been told that Hank and Willie were there every day helping in his absence. Allen was reluctant to consent right away, but two days after he could stay active for a whole day and attend to his studies, he let Charlie go back to work. He was pleased that his son was feeling such a sense of responsibility or that at least his normal energy had returned, and knew his reluctance was due to feelings of overprotectiveness after they'd had such a scare, but he was confident that Frank would keep Charlie's activity to a sensible level.

26

The Hero

Since there was no school until the first week of September, there were lots of children running around when Grace came into town that day for buttons and thread. Little Ruth Gilbert was drawing pictures with a stick in the dirt road, oblivious of the wagon that was barreling toward her. Grace was about to run out after her when she was snatched back and pushed out of the way. Her ankle hit a step and she fell back as she watched Frank pull his gun out and fire in the air as he charged in front of the horses. The startled animals veered off to the left, as the driver pulled up on the reins. But Ruthie, who was startled by the gunshot, was still standing like a statue in the road. Without missing a step, Frank holstered his gun, dove for Ruth, and rolled her out of the way just before the back wheel of the wagon passed the place where she had been standing.

Those who saw the incident rushed to see if the child was okay and congratulate Frank for his heroic act. The commotion brought the Perkins and Ruth's mother out of the mercantile. When she learned that her daughter's life had been saved, she cried and hugged Frank, saying, "Oh, Mr. Madison, how shall I ever thank you?" A crowd gathered around to pat him on the back and praise his bravery. Grace could tell Frank was embarrassed by all the attention. She chuckled to herself, got up, brushed off her skirt, and started walking home. *I'll wait until tomorrow to get the buttons and thread.*

Frank caught up with her when she was halfway home. He dismounted Pilot and fell in step with her. "Did I hurt you?"

"Not at all. I'm so glad you saved Ruthie. She's a quiet introspective little girl. I'm not surprised she didn't notice she was in danger. When she's engaged in drawing, she loses track of what's going on around her. It would have been a great loss to her family if she had been taken and, one day, I'm sure there will be a young man very grateful for her life." Grace stopped, turned, and smiled at Frank. She couldn't help putting her arms around his waist. He crushed her to him, as she whispered into his neck, "I love you."

"Grace," he responded, astounded by this confession. *Can it be true?* He tightened his hold on her to assure himself she was real and to keep his body from flying apart with the joy vibrating in every nerve. He kissed the top of her head, then her eyes, then her neck, and finally his lips captured her mouth. His heart was bursting with love for her. His kisses were wildly passionate. He didn't ever want to let her go, but Pilot, impatient with standing, nudged his back, throwing them off balance. Still holding her tightly, he said, "I asked your father weeks ago if I could court you. Neither of us was sure how you would respond, so I've been taking it easy. It's been hard. Grace, I'm not sure I can ever fully express what you mean to me."

"Well, Mr. Madison," she said, pushing back, and giving him a pat on his chest and an endearing smile, "I'll just give you some time to work on that." Then she turned to continue her walk home.

Overwhelmed by his emotions, Frank stood there watching her. His soul was on fire. Grace loved him. He thought about their conversation. *She praised me without making me feel one bit embarrassed. She's so wonderful.* He didn't know how anyone could love another person as much as he loved Grace. He knew his mind, body, and soul were hers, and she loved *him. Thank you, Lord. I'll take good care of her and be the best husband that has ever lived. Now that's putting the cart before the horse,* he chuckled to himself, when he realized his heart and mind were way ahead of their current circumstances.

27

Desperation Leads to Determination

When she measured out the spices for the stew she was making and it left the jar empty, Grace panicked. *What am I going to do? We didn't get the garden set up this summer and I need to learn more about the plants that grow around here.* She'd become avid about working with fresh herbs and found places where the plants were growing that Black Feather had shown her. She had collected a good supply, but would need many more varieties to make successful mixes.

The next morning, when she and Charlie were discussing his studies, she asked, "Charlie, would you be willing to cut your studies short today?" *Silly question.*

"Sure, what's up?" he answered.

"I don't need to go help Father today. Do you think Frank really meant it when he said we could ride his horses anytime?"

"Sure. Where do you need to go?"

"Do you remember where Black Feather's village is? I need you to help me find it. I know we'll be starting a lot later than we did the day we went there before, but it still stays light until almost eight. Since we've been exploring the country with Frank, I've gotten used to both the terrain and riding astride so I think we could travel faster than we did the first time we went. I need to find out more about the edible plants that grow around here."

"Rich and I have been out that way a couple of times. I'm sure I can find it," he answered.

"Okay, while you finish that assignment you are working on, I'll go over and saddle the horses and bring them back here. I think if we leave by nine-thirty, we can make it back before dark."

"What if Black Feather isn't there?"

"I'm going to take a jar of my seasoning blends with me. If he isn't there, maybe his wife will understand what I want if I show her the mixture and let her smell it. If she does the cooking, she probably knows as much as Black Feather about herbs and where to find them. I think I can get her understand what I want."

Charlie, although surprised that Grace wanted to ride out there without Frank, was delighted with the plan.

Since Grace could now easily sit astride, they were able to get to the Indian village much faster than their first trip. As they approached, Charlie felt a bit nervous. He wasn't sure anyone would remember them, but he was amazed at Grace's confidence. *Maybe it's because those spice mixes are so important to her.*

As soon as they reached the outskirts of the village, they dismounted and began to slowly walk toward the tepee they remembered belonged to Black Feather. The children stood still as soon as they spotted Charlie and Grace. Then one little boy said something and ran into Black Feather's tepee. Grace was relieved to see Black Feather come out. She smiled and waved. To her joy, he returned the gesture.

"I apologize for coming uninvited," she said, offering her hand. "My seasoning mixes are getting used up and I'm feeling concerned about replacing them."

"You are welcome to come anytime. I'm very glad I was here," he answered.

When they left hours later, Grace had both hers and Charlie's saddlebags filled with plants. She was delighted to have discovered that mint and allspice were two of the plants that were readily available. There were a couple of other plants she wasn't familiar with, but she looked forward to learning to use them.

It was already dark when Frank's house came into view, and they were both thankful for the lanterns he had burning.

"I'm glad we left him a note, Charlie. We spent much more time there than I planned, but I'm so delighted with all the plants I learned about today. Next summer we will have a wonderful garden."

"It might take more than one summer to get the plants established, sis, but this sure was a worthwhile day. Wasn't Black Feather nice? I wasn't sure about your wisdom going there without Frank, but you sure charmed him."

"I did no such thing, Charlie. Black Feather is a very kind person, and I think he's a natural teacher and appreciates our interest in the vegetation around here."

As they drew near Frank's house, her heart rate picked up. She knew it was caused by the anticipation of seeing him, but tonight there was something else. She had the oddest sensation of coming home. *Is this place actually my home now?* she wondered. She had so enjoyed the day and was surprised at how okay she was going to the Indian village on her own. *Well, I don't think I would have braved it without Charlie, but it wasn't at all like the first time.*

Her heart took flight when she saw Frank waving at them.

Richmond was very far away.

28

Disaster

It was Friday. Frank was in the bank withdrawing the payroll when he felt his chair vibrate. He instinctively knew what had happened.

"Put that money back in the safe, Mr. Johnson," he yelled, as he bolted out of the bank.

Luke Rogers was standing next to the door keeping a lookout for those strangers that were still in town. He jumped to attention when Frank came rushing out of the bank.

"Luke," Frank said, as he was mounting Pilot. "There's been a collapse in the mine."

Luke was on his horse in seconds. They were already heading toward the mine by the time the pillars of dust hit the town. Frank was glad the tremor had people frozen in their tracks. It made it easier for them to get through the town as they raced to the mine.

When they got there, men were already pouring out of the entrance. Frank jumped off Pilot, dropping his reins to the ground knowing the horse wouldn't wander. He saw Henry Caldwell first. He was holding his arm.

"Henry, was it your shaft?"

"No, it's B shaft."

"Okay, make sure everyone from A shaft is out, and then send Jack McDonald and Tom Daniels in after Luke and me if they aren't injured."

"Okay, boss."

Jack and Tom were strong and competent men, and Luke was an experienced miner. Frank knew these men would know exactly what to do. He threw off his hat, as he and Luke each grabbed a pick and a lantern.

As the men from A shaft were making their way out of the mine, Frank quickly checked each one. The vibration had disturbed some of the framework in A shaft causing some injuries but none were serious. Frank and Luke weren't more than thirty feet into B shaft before they came across the injured men making their way out.

"How far in is the collapse?" Frank asked Conrad Hall who was helping his partner.

"About ten feet past the new section."

Frank knew the new section was forty feet deep and most likely men were trapped behind the collapse.

"Dear God, please let them be alive."

Three more men were making their way out when Jack and Tom caught up with them. Frank was glad to see the next two men coming out had only minor scrapes. Next, they encountered Jeff Clarke who had an injured arm and Sam Martin who was helping his partner with an injured leg.

Willie had a young man draped over his shoulder but he didn't look in very good shape himself.

"Willie, how many men are behind the collapse?"

"Not sure, probably six or seven."

"Are there more injured men on this side?"

"Yes, I'm afeared most of them are hurt one way or another."

"Jack, I want you to go back and get six men to come in and help get the injured to safety. Luke, Tom, and I will work on getting the trapped men out."

"Right," answered Jack.

As they made their way further into the mine, Frank continued to inspect each injured man. Most had some kind of injury, a couple quite serious but no critical. He felt a prick of gratitude.

They worked their way through the fallen rocks until they got to the collapse. Frank took a minute to survey the situation. He saw that only two large stones were in the way; Most were of a size that they could easily pick away. However, he noticed some of the undisturbed walls might not hold once they started removing the stones blocking the passage.

"Tom, you and Luke go back and get some lumber to shore up this area before we start pulling these rocks away."

Knowing time was critical, both men hurried to carry out his request.

Frank continued to study the fallen rocks. He searched to find the easiest place to make an air passage. He listened. Even after calling out, he couldn't hear any activity on the other side of the collapse. It worried him.

*****

As Grace was standing in her father's office looking at Frank's file, she began to realize that all the land they had ridden on during their outings, with the exception of the Indian village, probably belonged to him. Then suddenly it seemed as if the world were breaking apart. She looked at her father.

"What was that?" she cried.

"I think it was probably the mine."

"The mine! Oh no!"

Grace was horrified. *Frank!*

Both she and her father put down the papers they were holding and ran out the door. There was gray dust filling the air and everyone was running in the direction of the mine.

"Grab a bucket of water on your way," yelled Hank as he, too, was running toward the mine.

Grace kept going, but her father ran back to the mercantile where the Perkins kept a stack of buckets just inside the door. He filled two up at the pump in front of the hardware store.

Grace was frantic. *Was Frank in the mine?* The thought of losing him made her sick. *Please, Lord, not Frank. Please, don't take Frank.*

When she got there, she looked around for him. She saw Pilot standing near the mine entrance, but Frank was nowhere in sight. Many of the men making their way out of the mine were injured.

The townspeople, along with the uninjured miners, were helping to take them to the grassy area in front of the mine to tend to their wounds. There was so much to do, Grace forced herself not to think about Frank. Sensing there would be a need for bandages, she stopped and started ripping the ruffles from her petticoat. When she had a handful, she ran from one person to another, passing out the cotton strips. She found her father was using his shirt to clean the wound of the man whose arm was bleeding. She stopped to help him. It was apparent that both this man and the one next to him had wounds that would need a real doctor, but she and her father knew they just had to do the best they could. Just then, Charlie came running up to them.

"Pa, what happened?" he yelled.

"There was a collapse in the mine," his father answered, not looking up from his task.

"Charlie, take Pilot and go back to the house and get my sewing basket and my medical bag," ordered Grace. "And hurry!"

Charlie took off without another word, just as another injured man was set on the ground beside them. Without a second thought, Grace lifted up her skirt and started tearing off more of her petticoat. This man had a head wound. At first, Grace was afraid he was dead, but then he moaned, so she wet the rag and started to clean his wound. Her father had the wound cleaned on the man with the laceration on his arm, so when Charlie returned with the medical bag and her sewing basket, she quickly threaded a needle and handed it to him. The other man lying near them had a broken leg. Charlie was still trying to catch his breath. Pilot was the fastest horse he had ever ridden. Grace ordered him to use the scissors and cut the pant leg of the man with the broken leg.

"Charlie, that man needs his leg stabilized. Do you remember reading how to do that?" she asked as she prepared to stitch up the gash on the other man's head.

"I think so," he responded.

"Well, do the best you can. There's no one else to help him right now." As she examined the wound on the man she was tending, she was glad to see it was only on his forehead and she wouldn't have to cut away his hair. The situation was so desperate she didn't stop to think about the gruesomeness of the task. She glanced over to see that Charlie was doing an excellent job of tending to the man with the broken leg. After cutting the pant leg off and seeing where the break was, he ran and found a couple of sticks, cut the pant leg in strips, and was using them to tie the sticks to his leg.

"Good job, son," his father said. "How did you know what to do?"

"I read about it in our medical book."

Grace heard this conversation and smiled. The man would need to have his bone set but she was glad Charlie was doing exactly what needed to be done for now to prevent further injury.

The whole area was in chaos. Frank was never out of Grace's thoughts, but there was so much to do she couldn't spend time looking for him. Besides, if he hadn't survived, she didn't want to know. The Perkins brought blankets from their store to cover the wounded men until their wounds could be attended to, while Hank was taking around water. The town didn't have a hospital and Grace had no idea how they were going to tend to all these injured miners, but everyone was doing what they could. Gradually, those with minor injuries were being escorted to their homes. Those with broken bones were being taken to the hotel. Joe Nelson had experience doctoring horses. He was the closest thing they had to a doctor. Grace hoped he was up to the task.

As the area was clearing, Grace saw Willie Barton lying up against a rock. His eyes were closed. She was afraid he was dead but went over to check on him.

"Mr. Barton," she said as she put her hand on his arm.

"Yeah," he answered.

"Where are you hurt?" she inquired.

"It's my shoulder," he said. "But I don't think it's too bad. I told them to take care of the others first."

"Let me look at it," Grace said. His shirt was blood soaked and the dried blood was sticking the shirt to his wound.

"Just a minute. I need to get some water so I can clean away the blood and the part of your shirt that is stuck to the wound." She tore some more fabric off her petticoat and wet it with a little trickle of water that was coming off the cliff nearby. As she started to pull his bloody shirt away, she winced. The wound didn't look good. The flesh was torn down to the bone. Grace almost lost her stomach.

"This cut needs to be cleaned really well before I can stitch it up, Mr. Barton," she explained. Willie only grunted. Grace had to use several strips of cloth to clean the blood and dirt away before she was finally satisfied the cut was clean enough to stitch up. As she spread on some Mercurochrome, she was sure this was a job for a real doctor, but like Charlie, Grace had studied the medical book and she knew it was up to her to help him. She prayed that she would be inspired beyond her own ability.

Because Willie's muscles were so tight, it took all her strength to hold the wound closed while she did the stitching. Since the cut was so deep, she put the stitches very close together and tied each one off separately, but she was still worried about them holding.

"Mr. Barton, you are going to have to refrain from using this arm for a while. This cut is very deep, so I don't think the stitches will hold unless you keep your arm immobilized." His reply was a deep groan. When she finished securing a sling made from what was left of her petticoat, she collapsed on the ground next to him. He pulled her over his chest with his good arm to protect her from the hard rock he was leaning against.

By the time the men who had been trapped behind the collapse were freed, it was evening. Since most of the miners in B shaft had been injured in one way or another, Frank was grateful the trapped men only had minor cuts and scrapes. He surveyed the area as he exited the mine. Some men were still being transported to their homes or the hotel. When he saw the chaos, he felt very thankful that the trapped men were some of the least injured and that they were able to get them free before the oxygen gave out. He was also grateful that, as they were pulling the collapsed rocks away, the tunnel had remained stable. But he was the most grateful they hadn't lost anyone. *That's a tender mercy, Lord. Thank you.* After it was obvious things were under control, he went back to check the condition of the mine. He would wire the Jackson Company a report to let them know what happened. He figured the mine would be closed for a while since it might take several weeks for an inspector to come and examine it. They might lose some of the men to the Turner Mine but, thankfully, it was payday and his men would have a month's wages in their pockets. Things would be hard for a while, and if the mine didn't eventually reopen, the whole town might be in trouble. In spite of this concern, Frank again thanked the Lord that he hadn't lost anyone.

As he came out of the mine, he reached down and picked up his hat, then looked around and saw Willie lying against a rock with Grace in his arms. A stab of jealousy hit him.

"Willie, what's this?" he said as he drew up to them.

"Gracie here sewed me up. I think it was hard for her. I couldn't see it, but she said it was a mighty nasty wound. She groaned quite a bit while she was doing the stitching, and when she finished tying this sling around my arm, she just collapsed. I don't think I was the first person she's helped today. The poor girl must be plum tuckered out."

"Wait here and I'll get someone to help you back to your place," said Frank.

"I'll be all right. Just lift the girl off me," replied Willie.

"Not on your life. You just stay put until I get you some help."

Willie tried to raise himself up in spite of Frank's command, then thought better of it when his head started spinning.

Frank saw Mr. Saulsby and Charlie heading toward them.

"I think we got everyone taken care of but Mr. Barton here," said Allen, as they drew up next to them.

When he saw the worried expression on Mr. Saulsby's face, Willie said, "Your daughter sewed me up. She's just plain wore out."

"How are you?" Allen questioned after being reassured that Grace was all right.

"I'm okay," said Willie. "I think you need a little help," responded Frank. "In spite of what you might think."

"You're probably right," he answered. "Missy here said I shouldn't move my arm."

"If you and Charlie can get him to his house, I'll carry Grace home," replied Frank.

171

Allen knew getting Mr. Barton home was a two-man job and that neither he nor Charlie could carry Grace as easily as Frank, so he agreed that following his suggestion was the best course of action.

*****

Frank was a bit puzzled when he picked Grace up. It didn't feel as though she was fully clothed. Then he remembered seeing all the bandages on the miners and the realization dawned on him that they must be wearing her petticoat. It made him chuckle. She was a unique and amazing woman. He recalled her concern about propriety when he carried her across the street last spring, but so much had changed over the summer. Since they had been going on their Saturday outings, he was sure she was getting more comfortable with life in Wylerton. And something had definitely changed since the day she and Charlie went to visit Black Feather on their own.

He wished he had seen her taking care of the injured. From Willie's remarks, his impression was that Grace had been both forthright and competent in assisting the wounded. It warmed his heart.

He thrilled at this chance to hold her in his arms again and pulled her closer, wishing for the day when it would be his right to always have her thus. Frank gave Pilot a whistle as he started walking Grace home. He was glad to see someone had neatly wrapped the horse's reins around his saddle horn. He knew he'd left them on the ground and was thankful there was plenty of grass in the area.

"Good boy," said Frank, as Pilot fell into step behind him. "Thanks for not wandering off."

Grace could tell her body was moving. She tried to wake up, but it felt as if she were made of lead. Then she recognized a feeling of warmth enveloping her. Even in her semi-conscious state, she knew she was safe and being protected. She snuggled comfortably into the arms of the person holding her and rested her head into the hollow of his neck. The feeling of his arms and something else seemed familiar, so even though she couldn't get her eyes to open, she knew it was Frank. *That means he's safe!*

Assured there was nothing wrong with Grace other than exhaustion, Frank was glad she wasn't conscious. He loved the way her soft relaxed body felt in his arms. She must have worked really hard to be this tired. He started thinking about this woman he loved and had cradled in his arms. She never seems to hesitate to take on new or difficult responsibilities or challenges. *It was generous of her to offer her services to Mr. Jenkins when Charlie quit going to school. I don't think she had ever done anything like that before. When we started our Saturday outings, she had to adjust to a new way of riding and handling the rugged terrain around here, but she never complained.* He realized how much he enjoyed watching her grow in her skill and confidence and was grateful that she and Tabby were bonding well. *It must have been hard for her to take over being the lady of the house after her mother died, yet she seems to be a very polished homemaker. I wish I had known her mother. She must have been a singular woman to have a daughter as capable and talented as Grace.* He wasn't surprised when Charlie told him about her drive for an education. *She pushes boundaries.* He was pleased with how dedicated she was to Charlie's education and smiled to himself about her bravery to seek out Black Feather because she was worried about her spice mixes. *Wylerton is so different from Richmond. Of course, it has been a big adjustment. It took me three years to learn a new way of life. Grace has been here less than a year and yet she has made so many adjustments. She is so different now from the uptight woman I carried across the street several months ago. In addition to the unexplainable draw I've had toward her right from the start, she is exactly the kind of woman I want to spend my life with. I can't wait for the day when she will be mine to take care of and protect.* Well, for now, he was free to hold her close to him. When he got near the house, he slowed down, becoming reluctant to give up the pleasure of holding and protecting her.

The house was dark, so he assumed Mr. Saulsby and Charlie hadn't returned yet. Frank reached down, opened the gate, and let Pilot into the yard. He walked up onto the porch and turned the door knob. It was locked. The moon wasn't up yet, but Frank could see the porch swing. He sat on it, shifting Grace's body so she was comfortably situated on his lap. He moved his arm from under her legs so he could hug her.

"Mmm," she said.

He was alone with Grace again. Her very presence was intoxicating. He pulled her into a snug embrace, kissed the top of her head, breathing deeply of the smell of her hair. It was sticky and dusty but it still smelled like her. He moved a strand of hair that had fallen across her face, then ran his hand down her cheek. Even with the layer of dirt from the day's labors, she was lovely. He moved his fingers up into her hair knowing it would further pull the pins loose, but he loved the feel of her hair and hoped its already disheveled state would be attributed to the day's activities and not his display of affection. He basked in the pleasure of feeling her slow even breathing against his neck.

Grace's body was without strength but she could smell and she smelled Frank. "You are safe," she whispered.

"Yes, but I'm not sure you are." He tightened his embrace, wanting to physically make her a part of him. She groaned.

"I'm sorry," he whispered, loosening his hold a bit.

Grace felt so secure in his arms. She used what little energy she had to snuggle against him. Her relief that Frank was okay was sending an overwhelming sense of warmth to her heart.

The moon had risen when Mr. Saulsby and Charlie were coming down the path. The porch was in shadow, but Allen thought he could make out some dark shapes on the swing. He smiled to himself, glad he had asked Frank to carry Grace home. The more he got to know Frank the more he liked him. Allen was sure Frank was a good match for his daughter. He had proven to be a good role model for his son. *Maybe moving to Wylerton wasn't such a bad thing after all.* He wasn't blind to the growing relationship between Frank and Grace and thought how apt Frank was in his courtship. It had been a long time since he had heard Grace either complaining or stamping her foot.

When they got to the house, Charlie gave Pilot a pat on his nose and tied his reins around the porch post.

"She's too tired to wake up," explained Frank when Allen and Charlie reached the porch. "I was hoping you would not be far behind me. I was a bit concerned when we got here and the door was locked. I hope fatigue is the only thing wrong with her."

"Thank you for bringing her home," answered Allen, as he placed the key in the door.

"Would you mind carrying her up to her room?" *I wouldn't mind carrying her anywhere,* he thought, but he said, "Thanks so much for your help today. It would have been a lot worse without the townspeople helping. I might have lost some of the men. As it is, I think everyone will pull through. I just hope Joe was able to handle the broken bones that needed setting."

"Yes, I counted at least four. I don't think the man's leg Charlie worked on was a very severe fracture. Let's hope none of them were any worse," said Allen. "What's going to happen to the mine?" he inquired, as they ascended the stairs.

"I don't know at this point," responded Frank. "I'm going to wire the company when I get back to town. They will probably instruct me to close it until they send some experts to inspect it."

Frank was pleased when he entered Grace's room. It was simple in its décor, but tasteful and not overly feminine. With the exception of a multicolored quit on the bed, the dominant white was offset by mute shades of blue and rust. Colors that complemented her personal appearance but not typically feminine. *Interesting that a woman as beautiful and feminine as Grace would have such subtle taste. I'm glad to see she doesn't go for frills.* He'd always associated frills with silly shallow girls whose minds didn't go beyond what dress to wear or how to talk sweetly. *Grace is not one of those girls.* His heart smiled. Another thing to love about her.

"Just put her on the bed," instructed Mr. Saulsby. "I'll take off her dirty clothes before putting her under the covers."

Frank did as he was instructed, unwillingly relinquishing his hold on her. She, too, wanted to protest, but there was no strength in her. She couldn't keep from drifting back to sleep. From the expression on Frank's face and in spite of her unconscious state, the feelings of affection going on between them were not lost on Allen.

"Are we going to work on your house tomorrow?" asked Charlie, interrupting Frank's desire to be the one taking care of Grace.

"Not tomorrow, Charlie," he replied. "I think we all need a rest. It's been a very strenuous day, don't you think?"

"Yeah, I guess."

"Well, you know the mine will probably be closed for a while. Why don't you come over a little earlier on Monday when you finish your studies and I'll bet we can make some real progress."

"Okay, that will be great," he said with a big smile.

Allen smiled at Frank and gave him a nod. He was sure Frank, unlike his son, realized how tired Charlie was. How tired they all were. After Frank left, Allen looked at his beautiful daughter. *I knew she would see behind the scruffy exterior. Frank is one of the finest and most capable men I have ever met.*

29

The Rough-Looking Men

Unknown to anyone but Mr. Johnson, Sheriff Singleton, and his deputy Mr. Downer, the Conner Gang was in jail. An experienced lawman, Sheriff Singleton had been concerned about the ruffians when, after more than two weeks, they were still just hanging around. He sent a wire to Denver inquiring about any outlaws that might be in the area. Although he wasn't sent any posters, the information he received about the Conner Gang made him suspect these men might be them. Since they hadn't broken any laws and were keeping a low profile, there wasn't anything he could do about their presence. However, he and his deputy stayed vigilant. As soon as the sheriff realized what had happened at the mine and that this would be the perfect opportunity for a bank robbery, instead of going to help with the disaster, he and Mr. Downer went straight to the bank, explained their suspicion to Mr. Johnson, and secreted themselves inside. As he suspected, the gang tried to rob the bank during the chaos resulting from the collapse at the mine. The sheriff and his deputy were fortunate to have caught them by surprise and had them all behind bars without a single shot being fired.

30

Frank and Charlie

With the outside of the house completed, Frank and Charlie were making good progress on the interior.

"What was your house in Richmond like?" asked Frank, as Charlie was handing him a piece of crown molding. "Well, it was a little bigger than this one. We had a parlor and a dining room, so we didn't eat in the kitchen, and we had servants' quarters on the lower level. There was a water closet and a bathing room on the main floor. And we had a laundry room like our house here does. (This description was settling Frank's concern about Grace being satisfied with his house.) It was right in town, so we didn't have much land around it like you have. There was a carriage house in the back and stables for the horses, but they weren't anything like your barn or the stables you plan to build. We had two carriages—one for my dad to drive to work and one for the family. Dad hired a boy to come every day to tend the horses, except for Bessey. She was Grace's horse, and Grace took care of her herself. She cried when she had to sell her."

"Yes, she told me about that."

"Bessey was a real pretty horse. I like Tabby better, though. Bessey was kind of a girlie horse. She didn't have spirit like Tabby."

"Do you think Grace likes Tabby?" asked Frank.

"Oh, you bet. She is always talking about how much she likes riding her and what a wonderful horse she is. I think she likes riding astride better than sidesaddle, too. She told me that she understands now why none of the women around here use a sidesaddle. Riding in a city like Richmond isn't the same as out here. This country is much more rugged, but I think she's gotten so she likes it and she is much better at it now. We made really good time the day we went out to Black Feather's village. I was so surprised she wanted to do that. But she's really worried about not having any spice mixes. She's like a chemist the way she likes to experiment with them."

"Yes, your sister is an amazing person. Does she ever talk about wanting to go back to Richmond?"

"Not anymore. She used to, but I think she is okay with living here now."

Naturally, this information pleased Frank. He wondered if Charlie knew how important it was to him to know how his sister felt about living in Wylerton.

"Charlie, I'm very glad you have been helping me build this house. When we started our Saturday outings, they were something I enjoyed too much to give up, so without your help, I don't think I would be getting it finished before winter."

"Well, I like helping you and I'm glad for all the things I'm learning. Helping you has been like getting a different kind of education. Books are fine, but I've discovered I like using tools and making things. Maybe someday I'll build my own house."

"I didn't think about that. I'll start teaching you more about why we're doing things the way we do. It could be a problem for you to not understand the basic principles behind good construction."

"Now you're sounding like my sister. She's always talking about how I should learn the reasons behind things."

"You have a pretty smart sister, Charlie. Don't ever hesitate to listen to her."

Maybe it wouldn't be so good for Frank to marry Grace. Then I'd have three people telling me what to do.

A week after the disaster, the mine was still closed. Frank and Charlie were working more hours on the house, and with Charlie's help, he was putting more of the finishing touches on the inside. He was glad Charlie's friend, Rich Davies, was coming over whenever he could. The boys would work until five, then go riding until just before dark. Charlie had basically taken ownership of Gray. Frank didn't discourage him. As his feelings for Grace grew and the love between them was becoming more sure, so were his feelings for Charlie. Charlie was becoming the brother he never had.

Although Willie, who was still recovering from his injuries, had been coming over, it was mostly for company. Grace had done a good job on his shoulder and it was healing well, but the wound still restricted the use of his arm.

"I'm sorry, I'm so useless," complained Willie, as they were all sitting around eating. "I'm glad you have Charlie here to help you. He sure is a fine boy. I guess he takes after his sister. She sure helped a lot of the injured men the day of the collapse."

When Frank learned about all that Grace had done to help that day, he wasn't surprised she had been so exhausted when he carried her home, or that she wanted to forgo last Saturday's outing.

"I had a similar wound, Willie. Don't get discouraged. It took me months to get my full strength back."

"Yeah, I guess you're right. I shouldn't complain. It's just that I've never been laid up before."

The next Wednesday evening, as they were finishing up the day's work, Frank said, "Charlie, let's take a break tomorrow. We are almost done, and I have some other things I need to do."

"Sure, should I come back on Friday?"

"That would be great, if you can."

Frank didn't tell Charlie he wanted to give him some time to relax. They had been working some long hours. He knew if he needed a break, so did Charlie. The boy had really stepped up to the work, but a break would be welcome and, for some reason, he felt an overwhelming desire to go fishing.

31

Saving Grace

Choosing to walk to the river, Frank started out at first light. As he was walking, he became aware of how odd it was not to be wearing his gun belt and chuckled when he remembered how uncomfortable it felt when he first put it on and how long it took him to get used to it. Now, he was very aware it was missing. His thoughts then turned to the Hartmans and their healing influence on his broken life. *They gave me a sense of life's value. Grace gives me a sense of purpose and self-worth.* (She was never out of his thoughts for long.)

I wonder what kind of person I would be if I'd stayed in Philadelphia? What would my life be if I'd never met Grace? She is so necessary to me. Dear Father in heaven, thank you for Grace. Were we destined to be together? How can another person be so much a part of my very soul?

When he got to the river, Frank noticed some good-sized fish were gathering in a little eddy on the other side, but he couldn't quite get his line over there. After catching a couple of smaller fish, he took off his boots and waded a little way into the water to get closer to where the larger fish were hanging out, surprised at how cold it was. *I hope I get a bite quickly. I'm not going to be able to stand in this water for long.*

*****

It was a perfect day. Grace decided to go to the woods on the other side of the river, hoping to find some elderberries and more herbs. Priscilla had given her a recipe for elderberry jam, and she was eager to try it. *Come, winter, it will be nice to have something other than strawberry preserves and apple butter, and maybe I can find some more herbs to make sure I have enough to last through the winter.* Now that she was getting more resigned to living in Wylerton, her thoughts about creating her own herb garden and planting some fruit trees were becoming more sure. *Several families have apple trees, so I'll find out if there are other kinds of fruit trees that would do well in this climate. The Davieses are generous about sharing their apples, but if I could plant a different kind of tree that would be nice for everyone, and next summer, with Charlie's help, I'll try my hand at gardening.*

When she got to the rope bridge, she noticed it looked a little lower than usual, but she couldn't tell if it was because the bridge was lower or the water was higher. She decided to try it. However, just as she was getting to the other side, the bridge gave away. Grace grabbed onto the railings as she was plunging into the cold water.

"Help!" she screamed. "Help!" It was a natural response, but as she was clinging to the ropes, she realized that there would be nobody around. As her skirt and petticoat became wet, their weight and the force of the water were making it harder to hold on, and she couldn't get her footing. As she squeezes harder on the railing ropes, she was seized by feelings of both desperation and hopelessness. Just as she was sure she was doomed to be washed down the river, she heard someone call her name.

*****

Frank had been at the river for about an hour. When he removed his boots and wading a little way into the water, he was able to catch two nice big fish. As he was putting the second fish into his basket, he was thinking the relaxation and his success were the reasons for coming to the river today. Then he heard a woman scream for help. He dropped his fishing pole and ran upstream, only to discover that it wasn't just any woman, it was *"Grace!"* The danger she was in threw his heart into his throat. He plunged into the water. It was running fast and up to his chest by the time he reached her. Its temperature was making it hard to breathe. He grabbed Grace around the waist and put his back to the current.

"Okay, you can let go now," he said.

"Are you sure?" she questioned. "My wet clothes are very heavy."

Frank realized she was right. He reached up with one hand and tugged on one of the ropes that was still attached to a tree. It seemed secure. Wrapping one arm around it, he pulled Grace closer against him. When he secured his footing, he said, "Okay, love. Now you can let go." Her hands were numb from the cold water, so when she let go, she didn't feel the pain of her torn flesh. Frank was saddened when he saw her bleeding hands, but he was grateful she had been able to hold on until he reached her. However, when she let go, he recognized immediately she was right about the drag of her wet clothes. They made it almost impossible for him to keep his own balance, much less be successful at getting her out of the water.

"You are going to have to undo your skirt and petticoat. Can you do that?" he asked.

"I'll try." Grace knew the situation was critical and that losing her clothes was less important than losing her life, and possibly Frank's. She instinctively knew Frank would sacrifice his life to save her, and the longer they were in the cold water, the greater the danger. She let go of the grip she had on his arm, hoping, as she worked on undoing her clothes, he wouldn't lose his hold on the rope or her, and they both end up being washed down the river.

As soon as they were unfastened, her clothing was carried off. Without that drag, Frank was able to stabilize his balance and, by keeping a grip on the rope, he helped her get her feet on the rungs of the broken bridge. She was then able to climb up onto the bank. Once she was on solid ground, Frank climbed out. Grace was sitting on the ground with her knees pulled up to her chin, rocking back and forth and shivering. Her soaking, wet clothes were virtually transparent, and her hair was falling down her back in a tangled mess. She looked so miserable. Without bothering to undo all the buttons, Frank quickly removed his wet shirt and handed it to her. It wouldn't be much protection for either her chill or her modesty, but he hope it would give her at least the illusion of propriety. She stood up. Frank turned his face as she pulled his shirt over her head and pushed her arms into the sleeves, but not before he caught a glimpse of her body beneath her wet clothes. She was so incredibly beautiful. He took a deep breath, steeling himself to behave like a gentleman. When she pulled his shirt down, she was grateful it reached almost to her knees, even though she was aware that it did little to actually reduce the appearance of her nakedness.

But the joy of being saved by Frank transcended her embarrassment. "Frank, how is it you are even here?" she questioned.

"I had the strongest urge to go fishing today. I told Charlie last night we needed to take a break. My precious love," he said, turning toward her and pulling her tightly against him, "I was so frightened when I saw you. What would I have done if I'd lost you?"

The panic he felt when he saw her desperately clinging to the ropes in the freezing water was still squeezing his heart. Grace saw the stricken look on his face. She hugged him with all her strength, in an effort to assure him she was okay. She could feel their hearts beating together. As she clung to him, she was suddenly aware what those fairy threads meant. She not only loved Frank, she belonged to him. She and Frank *were* destined to be together. She looked up at him, and they both came to the realization that they shared a sense of belonging. Consumed by the passion of their kisses, consciousness of everything else disappeared.

Frank was the first to come to his senses. "Come, Grace. I must get you home before you get chilled."

Chilled. What is he talking about? My whole body is on fire.

He stepped away from her and looked at her hands. The cold water had stopped the bleeding. Then he looked into her eyes and saw all that she was feeling—the fear of nearly drowning, the gratitude of being saved, and a love for him that she wanted to express. He drew her back into his arms and smothered her again with kisses. It took him a few more minutes to break their heated exchange. He took a deep breath. Even with her clothes beginning to dry, he could see how beautifully feminine she looked and felt.

"I love you, Grace," he said, pulling her tightly against him again. "But what I feel is way beyond what those words express."

"You've said that before. Now I understand how you feel. Oh, Frank," she said, still clinging to him. "I love you so much. I think perhaps, even when I first met you, I felt as if I belonged to you, but I didn't understand how that was possible. I didn't even know you." She wondered if she should tell him about the silken threads she'd been experiencing, but from the look on his face, decided another time would be better. She perceived his complex emotions fluctuating between his waning panic when he saw her clinging to the broken bridge, desire aroused by their physical closeness (it was being so hard for *her* to think of anything but touching him), and his new concern of getting back across the river. He might think her delirious if she started talking about imaginary silk threads.

"Since the terrain is less steep upstream, I think if we walk up that way we can find a better place to cross the river," he suggested, holding her at arm's length.

Grace looked at the scar on his shoulder. *I wonder how he got that.* But instead of asking, she said, "Thank you for lending me your shirt." But since he was holding her away from him, and she was no longer feeling the warmth of his body, she realized without his shirt, he, too, would be feeling cold and recognized the need to get moving. She turned to start walking, but after taking a few steps, she said, "Wait a minute. I want to dump the water out of my boots." Frank was standing behind her, admiring the beauty of her hair falling over her back when he heard her making a strange sound.

"Grace, are you all right?" he asked, worried that her emotions were out of control.

"Yes," she responded.

"Are you *laughing?*"

"Yes, I was just remembering this isn't the first time we've been in this situation."

"What?" he responded.

"Both of us soaking wet, and you with no shirt."

"Yes, I remember," he said, chuckling, "but the difference is, this time, love, we're on the wrong side of a river and not yet out of danger. So I think we'd better hurry and get moving. The temperature will drop with the sun."

Grace was sobered by the urgency in his voice. When she finished tying the laces on her boots, he extended his hand to help her stand. She didn't hesitate for a moment. She knew very well the minute she touched him again she would feel those silken fairy threads that had become so familiar, and now that she recognized they were weaving her soul to his, she welcomed them. *So you have been trying to tell me I belong to Frank.* She smiled at this understanding. She looked at Frank and smiled at him. The love she was feeling warmed her very soul, and she wished she would never have to let go of him.

The feel of her soft, warm hand sent a thrill up Frank's arm, but he was mindful of her wounds, so he held it softly and resisted the urge to gather her back in his arms.

"Come on, love," he said, barely able to speak. His chest so swollen with emotion and concern for Grace. "Let's look for an easier place to cross."

The area was strewn with fallen trees and branches. To keep her mind off their precarious situation, Grace began to share her feelings, wondering why it was something they seldom did on their Saturday outings. Perhaps because Charlie was always with them, or because there were so many other interests demanding their attention.

"Do you know I have always felt at home in your arms? I was incensed that time you carried me across the street before we knew each other, but I was also confused because being in your arms made me feel so secure and when you put me down, I felt abandoned. I couldn't understand it. You have driven me to stamping more than once, you know."

"I know," Frank answered, smiling. "Charlie told me about your stamping." His mind scanned all he'd been learning about Grace over the summer. He was happy with all of it, even the quirky things like her foot stamping. Realizing how complete his love was heightened his anxiety.

"Let's keep moving Grace. We need to get back across this river soon," he said, urging her on, but at the same time being mindful not to go faster than she was able. He was grateful for her chatter. It helped keep his mind off the almost panic swirling in his brain. Their danger wasn't over by a long shot.

Grace smiled at his knowing about her stamping, glad it didn't put him off. She looked at him walking in front of her. He was so beautifully built, seeing him without a shirt aroused feelings of desire that were almost scary in their intensity. She wished they could stop for a minute so she could put her arms around him again and feel his bare skin. She thought his scruffy hair and beard were an odd contrast to his smooth skin and well-defined muscles. Even the scar across his shoulder that extended down onto the right side of his chest didn't detract from his beautiful masculine physique. *I want to belong to him. Oh, how I want to belong to him.* Even though they were beginning to dry, Grace knew when her clothes were wet she was entirely immodest, even after putting on Frank's shirt. Now as she observed how his priority was to get them to safety, it brought a clear realization to her—Frank was ever the gentleman he'd more than once proved himself to be.

Frank could feel the temperature dropping and the danger of them getting hypothermia rising, so by forcing himself to concentrate on the situation at hand, he kept his mind off Grace's beauty and the desire aroused by knowing she shared his feelings.

"I hope we don't come to an impasse before we find a good place to cross," he said.

"Are you all right?" questioned Grace. "At least I have shoes."

"I'm fine. At one point on my way out here from Philadelphia, my horse got a sore foot, so I decided to walk, hoping that it would heal faster. My boots were so worn I found it better to walk barefoot."

Grace realized there was still a lot she didn't know about Frank, especially about his experience coming to Wylerton.

"We've never really talked about how you got to Wylerton. How long did it take you?" she inquired.

"Three years. I wasn't in a hurry. Once I got west of the Appalachians, I was blessed to meet people who helped me and taught me things I needed to learn about living in the West. I stopped in a lot of places to learn the skills I would need to survive alone in the wilderness. I spent a year in St. Louis and worked in a bank. During my time in St. Louis, I spent the weekends learning to use my gun and practicing to live off the land. That's where I developed the ability to hear sounds others usually fail to notice. It saved my life on more than one occasion. That's why I knew that Mountain Lion had come up on us."

"Well, you most certainly saved our lives that time."

I hope I can do it again, he thought as the seriousness of their current situation pressed upon him. He knew he could survive crossing in the deep cold water again, but he wasn't so sure how well Grace could.

"Oh, so you were a banker?" Grace questioned, breaking into his thoughts. "My father owned a bank in Richmond."

"I just worked as a teller for a year. I got the job because of my degree in accounting." Frank thought back to the many young girls that had come into the bank during the time he spent in St. Louis. *Some were very pretty, but I wasn't drawn to any of them the way I was to Grace the first time I saw her in church, or the day I followed her into the mercantile. Even though her mood wasn't welcoming, there had been something that pulled me to her.* He reflected on the overwhelming connection he felt to her now and was glad he hadn't been discouraged by their rocky start. *Look where we are now. Grace is my whole reason for living.* "That experience and my degree is how I ended up running the mine," he continued. "Most of my responsibilities are managing the finances and the payroll."

"That's why you wear a gun?"

"Partly," he answered. "While I was traveling across the country knowing how to use it was necessary to protect and feed myself. I got used to wearing it, and it does make people think twice about giving me trouble."

Grace smiled, reminded again at what an awe-inspiring person Frank was. She remembered the day he taught her how to shoot and, after seeing him use his gun a couple of times, knew he had exceptional skill. They walked silently for a while. Frank was concentrating on their situation, hoping they would soon find a good place to cross. Grace was struggling, finding it hard to keep her footing on the uneven, cluttered terrain and her mind off the dangerous situation they were still in, but she didn't complain. Her thoughts wandered back to her life in Richmond. *Yes, how different life is here. Now that*

I have Frank, would I want to go back? She decided she just wanted to be home, but that no longer meant Richmond.

"After you told me how you lost your family, I remember reading about that accident in the newspaper," she said, picking up the conversation. "I haven't handled my loss nearly as well as you, and I still have part of my family. I hope you know how much I admire you. I'm ashamed at what a gloomy person I've been. Also, do you know how helpful your influence on Charlie has been? When he finally decided to let me teach him, I was worried that he would be resistant, and it would take all the fun out of it. But he wants to be like you, so he dives into his studies with real enthusiasm. As a result, we have some wonderful discussions. One of the things I missed the most when we moved here were conversations about the things we were studying that I used to have with my mother and my friend Caroline. Since I couldn't go to college, my friend Caroline and I would study college courses on our own. My mother was so good to encourage us and participate in our discussions. I had a very close relationship to her, which is one of the reasons I was extremely devastated by her death. There are times I still have to work on getting over it."

Although Charlie had already talked to Frank about her drive for education, he was pleased that Grace was sharing this information. It made him aware that finding her had done a lot toward helping him come to terms with losing his family, and realized that now he perceived Grace as his family and wondered if that had been the case the first time he saw her. That memory was so vivid. He was sitting in the back of the church when the congregation started standing after the sermon. Grace turned her face toward him, and he felt his heart immediately respond to her. At the time, he thought it was because she was so beautiful. But the day he followed her into the mercantile, he knew there was something else drawing him to her, something he wasn't sure he fully understood even now. For the present, he was glad to listen to her talk while he concentrated on getting them back to safety.

They had been making their way up the river for quite a while, and it was becoming obvious to Frank they weren't going to find an easy place to cross soon enough. Even though their clothes were dry-ing, the sun had dipped behind the mountains, and the temperature was dropping fast. His anxiety started rising. He could feel Grace struggling even though she hadn't complained. She was stumbling more, and her grip on his hand was getting tighter. He knew her constant chatter was an attempt to keep from causing him any more worry. He remembered seeing a place a few yards back that was rocky but much more shallow. The water was moving fast over the rocks, but he thought if he carried her, he would be able to navigate it.

"Grace, we should go back a ways. We passed a place that I think I can cross if I carry you."

"Okay, if you think that's the best thing," she replied.

The sound of her voice told Frank she was tiring. He prayed he hadn't been wrong about the spot they were heading back to. When they finally got back to it, it didn't look as easy as he had remembered, but under the circumstances, he thought it was their best option. He knew they were running out of time.

"This is it," he said.

Grace looked at the river.

"Are you sure?" she questioned.

"I think so. Let's just hope I'm right. The water is somewhat shallow here. I think the worst that can happen is that we fall and get soaked again, but I'm sure we can make it across."

Grace looked at him. She could see both concern and determination in his worried blue eyes. She decided to trust the determination. She put her arms around his neck so he could pick her up and immediately felt secure. *Oh, how I love this man.*

Thinking she was afraid, Frank said, "Don't worry. I won't let go."

Neither will I, she thought.

"Frank, are you sure you want to carry me?"

Without voicing his wish to keep her out of the cold water, he answered, "Yes, I think it will be easier if I just concentrate on where I'm putting my feet instead of worrying about both of us."

"Well, if you are sure."

"I am."

When he lifted her legs off the ground, she pulled herself closer and clung tightly to him. Frank paused a second to settle his heart rate before stepping into the water. Even though her clothes were getting dry, he could feel her soft body through them. She felt so delicious his heart was overflowing, knowing someday she would be his. *She loves me!* This reassuring knowledge would have made for complete satisfaction if it weren't for their dire situation.

The water was moving faster than he anticipated. His feet and legs were immediately chilled by the cold water. His pants protected his legs somewhat, but his feet were soon very uncomfortable. However, by being careful, to make sure each foot was in a secure place before picking up the other, he got them safely across, but his feet had gotten quite numb. Grace didn't release her hold on him, so he continued to carry her as he started back down to the bridge and the trail that led to her house. He hoped his numb feet wouldn't cause him to stumble. *I'm grateful I carried her, he thought, in spite of the discomfort to my feet. I know even wearing shoes her legs and feet would have suffered from the cold water. Besides it is always an extraordinary privilege to hold her.*

The thought crossed Grace's mind that since she was wearing shoes she shouldn't be letting Frank carry her, but the stress of the day was setting in and she couldn't give up the safety and comfort of his arms.

"Grace, are you all right?" he asked.

"No," she replied. He gave her a squeeze. She lifted her face to him. The kiss was inevitable. When their lips parted, both had eyes sparkling with love. Grace nestled her face against his neck. He continued walking back toward the trail that lead to her house.

From the encroaching darkness, Frank knew it was way past the time when she would have returned home and that her father was probably fretting. It was slow going with his numb feet, but feeling the need to be careful, he only moved as fast as he could, without stumbling. He was glad there was a well-worn path from the bridge. Once there, he would be able to walk much faster.

Grace kept a tight grip on Frank for the first little while, but when she relaxed, he guessed she had fallen asleep. The warmth of his arms and the steady rhythm of his body as he was carrying her allowed her to let go of the anxiety of the day. She gave up her fear of drowning when Frank had a hold of her in the river, but the stress it had caused and the ensuing trouble getting back across the river had taken their toll. However, as she began to relax a little her thoughts turned again to the trouble carrying her might be causing Frank until she remembered what kind of man he was—a strong protective gentleman. *The water is so cold, I wonder how his feet are*, she thought, but his gait was steady, his breathing normal and this, along with the pleasure of being held by him, caused her to let go of her anxiety, and wish she could stay in his arms forever.

When they were in sight of the house, Frank saw Mr. Saulsby running to meet them. He was aware that they were a strange sight—him with no shirt or shoes on. Grace with only half of her clothes. He was going to have to do some quick explaining. When Mr. Saulsby was within earshot, Frank said, "The rope bridge broke. I was fishing downstream when I heard a yell for help. Thankfully, she had grabbed onto the bridge ropes, but her clothes were pulling her down. When I got ahold of her, I couldn't lift her out of the water. By having her take off her skirt, I was able to get her out, but we were on the far side of the river, and it took us a while to find a place to cross. It's been quite a day for her Mr. Saulsby. Except for the rope burns on her hands, I think she's all right, although she might be in a state of shock."

If he hadn't been so relieved to see Grace being safely returned to him, Allen would have been amused at Frank's hasty explanations.

"Frank, I can't thank you enough," he said, taking Grace in his arms. "I can only imagine what would have happened if you hadn't been there."

"Yes, sir."

"Oh please, call me Allen. Considering our understanding and all you've done for Charlie and now saving Grace, I don't think we need to be so formal."

"Ask him to come to dinner on Saturday, Father," Grace whispered in her father's ear.

"Yes, it's the least we can do. Please join us for dinner on Saturday, Frank."

"Thank you. It would be my pleasure."

"Until then." Allen smiled at Frank as he turned toward the house with Grace in his arms. Frank didn't know how long he stood there, watching Grace's father carry her away. He was only aware of how alone he felt. He wasn't just in love with Grace; his need for her was all-consuming. With her, he felt complete.

When she was almost out of sight, he shook himself and headed back to the river to get his boots and fishing gear. As he looked at the two large fish he caught, he remembered how pleased he had been at his success. That seemed ages ago. He sat on the riverbank, letting tears of gratitude run down his cheeks as he thanked the Lord that he hadn't lost her. When he got back to his house, he was glad he had a working fireplace. It was going to take some effort to warm up his feet and get his body temperature up to normal.

*****

The next day, it was hours past noon by the time Grace woke up. Both her father and Charlie were long gone. She got out of bed, taking her quilt with her, dreading the thought of being cold. She walked into the kitchen but wasn't interested in eating, so she opened the door and stepped out onto the porch. What a wonderful sight—the mountains dressed in their fall colors, the sun bouncing off their barren tops. She watched the meadow grass swaying in the soft breeze. *This is certainly a beautiful place,* she thought.

*****

When Charlie got to Frank's house that afternoon, he saw him sitting on the porch swing with his feet wrapped in a blanket.

"Hi, Charlie," he said. "How is your sister today?"

"She was still sleeping when I left, but I think she is okay," he answered.

I hope so after the trauma of yesterday, thought Frank. He hoped she wouldn't suffer any long-term effects. He knew experiences like that could have dramatic consequences. He prayed the experience wouldn't cause her to be discouraged about living in Wylerton again. *I know she hated it when she first arrived, but I think our Saturday outings and her other experiences have changed that. Please, Lord, don't let her want to leave here.*

"Well, my feet are not in the best shape today," said Frank. "They aren't quite recovered from walking barefoot and wading the cold water. I'm going to take it easy for a couple of days. If you can put the doorknobs on the upstairs doors, we'll call it good for today. They are in a box on the kitchen table."

"Sure," answered Charlie.

"And, Charlie, let's give tomorrow a rest too. I've been invited to join your family for dinner on Saturday, and I want to be in good shape when I get there." He planned to get a haircut, and he decided it was time to shave his beard. He didn't know how Grace would react to the prominent scar on his jaw, but it was time he found out. She hadn't made any comments about the scar on his chest, but they'd both had other things on their minds at the time.

Once Charlie was upstairs, Frank's thoughts returned to all the things he knew about Grace: her drive to be educated, her interest in being useful, and her creativity. He thought how hard it had been for her to lose her mother and then get transplanted into a totally different world. *She might not recognize it, but she has weathered that hardship and tragedy and is becoming better for it. No, Grace will be okay. And now she has me. I hope she really understands how much she means to me and knows I will always protect her and keep her safe.* Then he silently thanked God again that he had been there for her yesterday. He shook himself at the memory of how close he'd come to losing her.

32

Revelations

Saturday afternoon, Grace was in the kitchen making sure everything was perfect. It was a beautiful warm day, so she was wearing her green sprig muslin dress. There were several times before that she had almost worn it but changed her mind, thinking it was too dressy for Wylerton. But this was a very special occasion and she wanted to look special. When she heard the knock on the door and her father say, "Come in, Frank," her heart jumped. She quickly removed her apron and rushed into the parlor, only to stop short when her eyes took in the incredibly handsome man standing in front of her. Her hands flew up to her face to cover her blush. "Oh," she said, then stamped her foot and ran into the kitchen and out the door.

"I'm sorry, Frank. I don't know what's gotten into her," Allen said as he headed for the kitchen. Grace had left the kitchen door open. Her father stopped there and watched her run to the cottonwood tree and throw herself on the ground. It dawned on him that she had never seen Frank without a beard and he remembered a conversation he'd had with her weeks ago.

"I just don't understand why Minnie and Priscilla are so taken with the Clarke brothers. They are so conceited and shallow. I think it's more important for a man to be average looking, have the qualities of a gentleman, intelligence and depth of character," she had said.

Well, Frank is anything but average-looking, thought Allen.

Sad at heart, thinking Grace was appalled by his scar, Frank was regretting having shaved his beard. Still, he knew he would have had to reveal it at some point.

"I know it's an ugly scar," he said, as Mr. Saulsby returned to the parlor.

Allen smiled. "It's not your scar that sent her flying, son. It's your handsome face."

"What!"

"She had no expectation of you being so good-looking. Go out there and talk to her. I'm sure you can straighten this out."

Grace was lying on the ground with her hands over her eyes. Frank paused at the kitchen door. Her dress. The girl in Richmond had been wearing the same kind of dress. The image of the girl walking down the street in a pine green dress had stayed vivid in his memory. *The same dress? Could it truly have been Grace?* The incident came flooding back. The way Grace moved. The effect she had on him. But he hadn't ever made the connection and still occasionally wondered if he would ever know who that girl was. Now seeing Grace in that dress, he was sure. His mystery girl and his true love—both were Grace. *We are meant to be together!* The joy of this realization welled up in his heart and made his chest ache.

When he drew close, he heard her sobbing.

"Grace, are you upset with me?"

"No."

"What's the matter, then?"

"The way you look."

"You're repulsed by my scar."

"No, your beauty."

"You're repulsed by my beauty?"

"Yes. Well, I mean, no. You've always looked so shaggy, I just wasn't expecting you to be so beautiful."

He chuckled. He was reminded of one of the things he admired about Grace. She didn't flaunt her own beauty or use it to attract attention. He'd often wondered if she even realized how beautiful she was.

"Grace, look at me," he said, as he knelt down and turned her over so he could see her face.

When their eyes met, he said, "Grace, can you still love me even if I look different than what you expected? I don't feel like a whole person without you. I need you. I hope you can accept the way I look. We are meant to be together, you know."

"Yes, I know."

Frank said, "When I was living in Philadelphia, I would go to Richmond to get brass fittings and deliver carriages. The last time I was there, while I was loading some boxes of hardware into my wagon, a girl walked past me. Her skirt brushed across the back of my legs. My heart skipped a beat. I was puzzled by my reaction to her touch. I watched her walk down the street. She moved like a dancer. I didn't ever see her face, but for some reason, I was affected by just the touch of her dress. Grace, that was you. You were that girl. I've occasionally wondered about her and sometimes hoped you were her, but I didn't know until I saw you in this dress. This was the dress you were wearing that day. I was drawn to you back then before I even knew you. I was also drawn to you the first time I saw you here in Wylerton. Since then, you have enchanted me, puzzled me, made me miserable, captured my soul, and given me a reason to live. The way you look, the way you move, the things that interest you, your idiosyncrasies, everything about you resonates with me. Now that I know you are also my mystery girl, I can't even begin to express the gratitude I feel for having been so blessed to find that you and she are the same person."

"Oh Frank," she said, smiling into his wonderful shining eyes. "But the first time I saw you, you scared me. I couldn't understand how a scruffy-looking stranger could make me feel as if I belonged to him. I kept feeling these silken threads that seemed to be attaching you to me, and they frightened me. I tried to avoid you, at first, but when those feelings wouldn't go away, I decided to get to know you better. In fact, I'm also sure there is something unique about our love. I've never had the kind of feelings about another person that I have for you. I, too, have such an overwhelming need for you. So I'm also sure that we belong to each other."

"Then marry me!" he said, as he took possession of her lips.

Her arms went around him and she pulled herself tight against him. When she felt their hearts beating together, she knew she was home.

Frank put his hands on each side of her head to deepen his kiss. The passion he had been holding in check for months was released, and her answer to his proposal was expressed as she returned his demanding kisses. Both felt the same sense of belonging. They couldn't get enough of each other.

"I saw this coming weeks ago," Charlie said, as he and his dad watched the lovers from the kitchen window.

"So did I, son," said Allen. "And I couldn't have wished for a better man for Grace. I guess we might as well eat our dinner while it is still warm. Who knows how long those two will be out there."

"Yeah," replied Charlie. "I'm starving."

Neither seemed concerned that Grace and Frank were sitting on the ground in a display of passion.

With dinner forgotten, Frank and Grace sat under the cottonwood tree, wrapped in each other's arms, basking in the joy of their new commitment.

Frank's heart filled with gratitude for having found Grace to be both the girl in Richmond and his true love. *Me from Philadelphia and her from Richmond, what are the odds that we would come together here in Wylerton?* he wondered. *Then again, maybe God, knowing we are meant to be together, had a hand in our destiny.*

Finally, he said, "I was worried you would be repulsed by my scarred face."

"Tell me how it happened."

"My horse stumbled on a bad section of the trail I was taking out of the Appalachians. A tree broke my fall and saved me, but gouged my face and my shoulder. I found my way to a ranch. The rancher, Bill Hartman, sewed up my wounds and he and his wife, Maggie, took care of me until I got my strength back. The scars look better now, but for a long time, they were pretty raw. I grew a beard to cover the one on my face. I was afraid people would be put off by the look of it."

"Frank, you are still so handsome, I can't imagine how intimidating your looks were before you got that scar."

"You think I would have been intimidating?" *I wonder if I should tell her how girls used to throw themselves at me?*

"Yes. The scar makes you look human and a little less like a Greek god."

Frank chuckled at her estimation of him. *When she looks in the mirror, does she not see the face of a goddess? Her humility—another thing to love.* "Grace, if my scar helps you to not be intimidated by my looks, I'm glad for them."

"You are still beautiful, you know."

"You mean handsome, don't you? Men aren't beautiful."

"You are," she replied, smiling at him.

Frank looked into her expressive hazel eyes and was glad she loved him even if he was *beautiful*. He took possession of her delicious mouth again.

After a while, Frank took her by the hands and raised her off the ground. "I thought you adorable the first time you stamped your foot at me. I will always think you are adorable," he said, as he pulled her tightly into another embrace.

"I'm building the house for you, you know. Did you guess when I asked you what color I should paint it?"

"Not really. I just figured you wanted a woman's opinion."

"Not just any woman's opinion, Grace. But your opinion I will always value. However, we don't have to live here if you don't want to."

"Frank, I love the house, I love you, and if you are in Wylerton, then it's home," she replied. This warmed his heart.

"You know I'm planning to raise and train horses."

"I would love to learn how to do that. It would be wonderful having you teach me. We could work together."

"So you would like that, would you?" he said, smiling. "You're aware, aren't you, that Tabby is already yours?"

"Is she?" said Grace with a shy smile on her face.

"Oh Frank, when can we get married?" she asked.

"I need a little more time to finish the house and you will need time to get ready for the wedding, won't you?"

"I suppose. But in the meantime, may I kiss you whenever I want to?"

"Only if you grant me the same privilege."

They decided to take immediate advantage of this agreement.

The Afterward

Sometimes two people are meant for each other and fate or whatever you wish to call it works with the circumstances of their lives to bring them together. Frank finding Grace was just such a circumstance. I quote from chapter eight in Jane Austen's *Persuasion*, "There could have been...no tastes so similar, no feelings so in unison, no countenances so beloved."

About the Author

Vicki Machoian was born in Washington, DC, and grew up in Wheaton, Maryland. She is a graduate of Brigham Young University where she majored in visual art and minored in English Literature.

After raising seven children, she became a teacher, a visual artist, and, upon discovering she loved working with clay, a potter. Although still a mother, grandmother, and great-grandmother, after retiring from teaching, she found time to indulge in her love of reading. Having never forgotten a comment made by a high school friend that "everybody has at least one book in them," she decided to test that theory. *Frank Finds Grace* is the result. However, since more stories are still swirling around in her brain, she may have stumbled onto a new career.

Vicki lives in Provo, UT, where friends and family know a gift from her probably means getting a piece of handmade ceramics or, in the future, one of her books.

CPSIA information can be obtained
at www.ICGtesting.com
Printed in the USA
JSHW032328211220
10467JS00001B/3